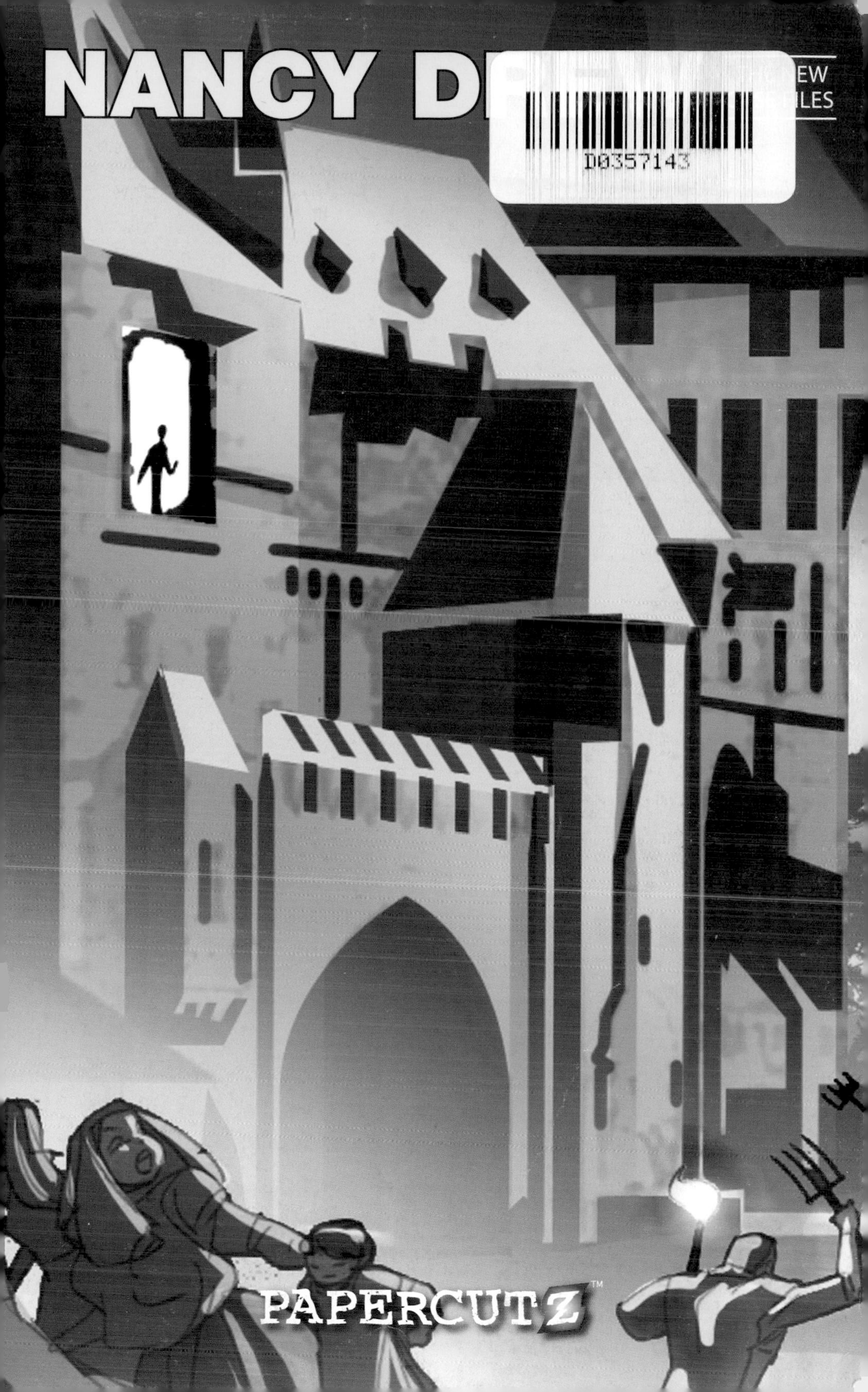
NANCY DR
EW
ILES
PAPERCUTZ

NANCY DREW GRAPHIC NOVELS AVAILABLE FROM PAPERCUTZ

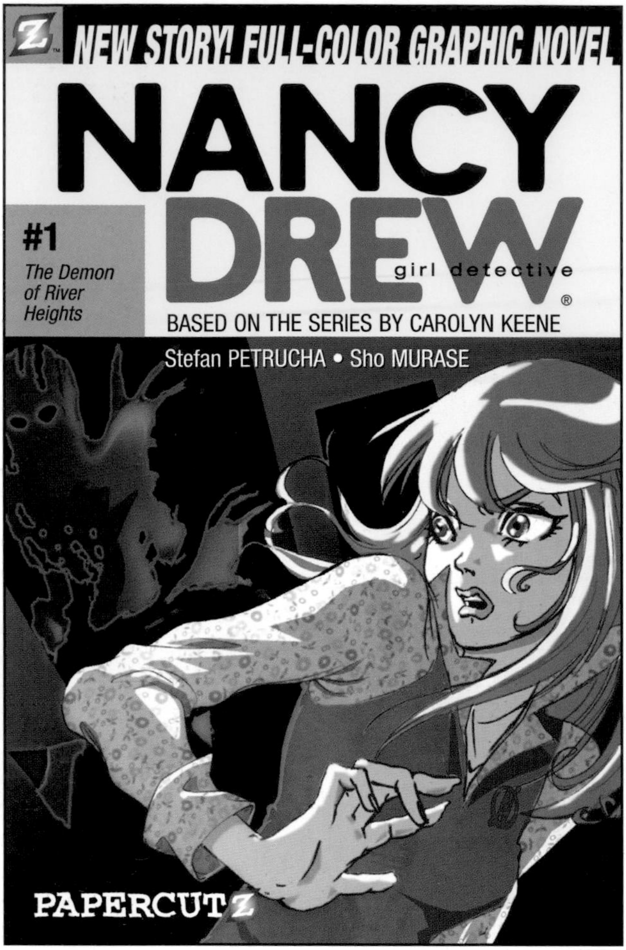
NEW STORY! FULL-COLOR GRAPHIC NOVEL
NANCY DREW
girl detective
#1
The Demon of River Heights
BASED ON THE SERIES BY CAROLYN KEENE
Stefan PETRUCHA • Sho MURASE
PAPERCUTZ

#1 "The Demon of River Heights"

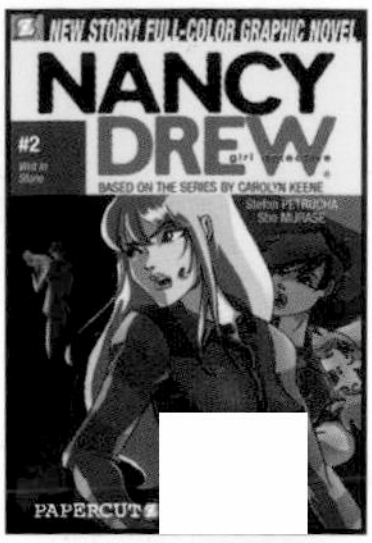
NANCY DREW

#2 "Writ In Stone"

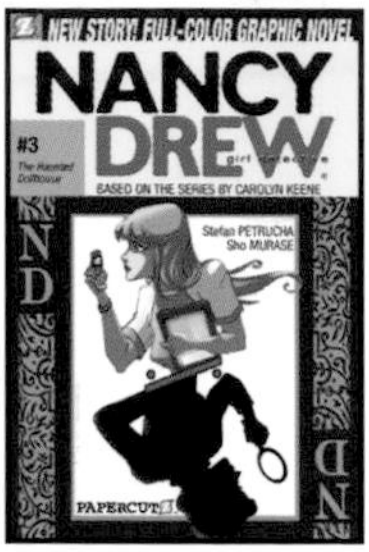
NANCY DREW

#3 "The Haunted Dollhouse"

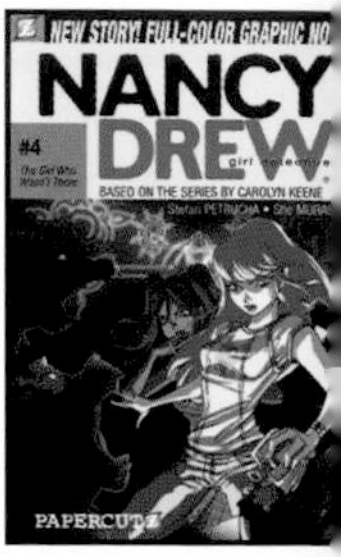
NANCY DREW

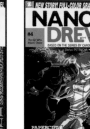

#4 "The Girl Wh Wasn't There"

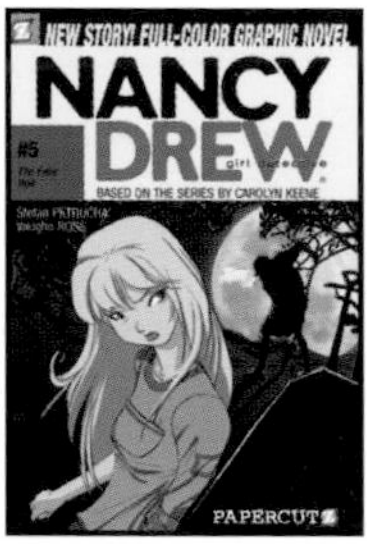
NANCY DREW

#5 "The Fake Heir"

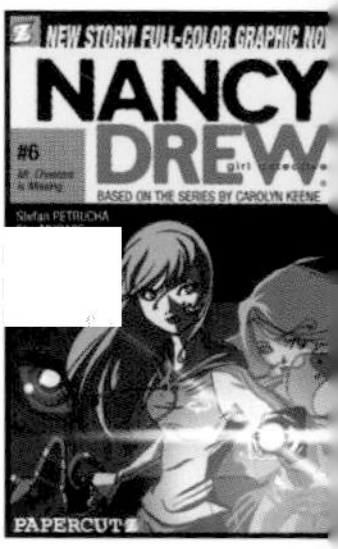
NANCY DREW

#6 "Mr. Cheeters Is Missing"

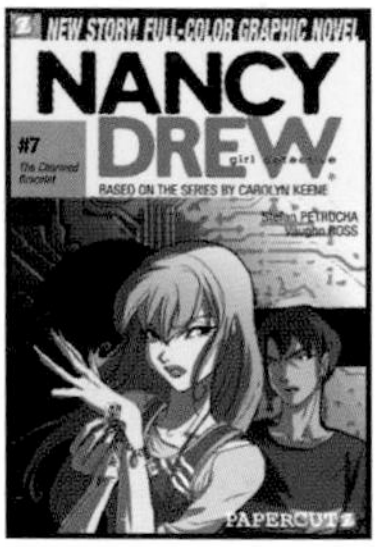
NANCY DREW

#7 "The Charmed Bracelet"

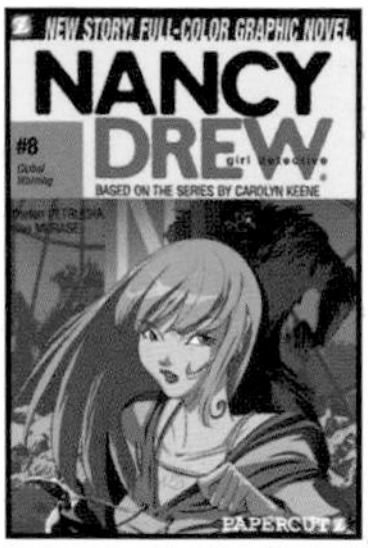
NANCY DREW

#8 "Global Warning"

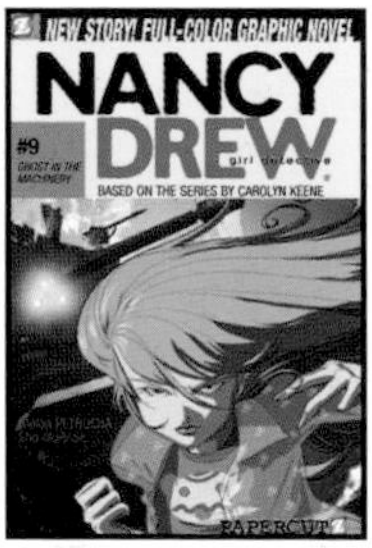
NANCY DREW

#9 "Ghost In The Machinery"

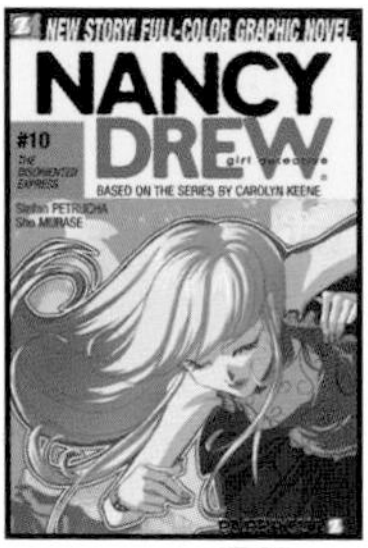
NANCY DREW

#10 "The Disoriented Express"

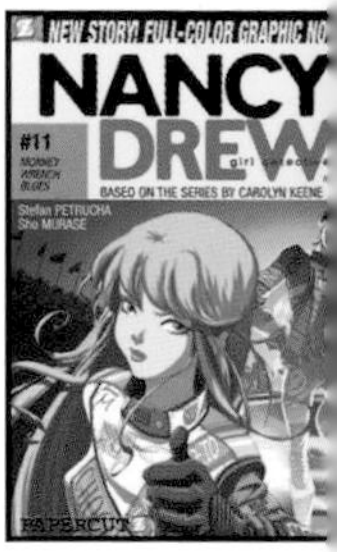
NANCY DREW

#11 "Monkey Wrench Blues"

Graphic Novels are $7.95 in paperback, $12.95 hardcover. Please add $4.00 for postage and handling for th first book, add $1.00 for each additional book. Please make check payable to NBM Publishing. Send to:

Papercutz, 1200 County Rd. Rte. 523, Flemington, NJ 08822, 1-800-886-1223

www.papercutz.com

rucha, Stefan.
cy Drew, vampire
yer. Part two/
10.
05222462818
01/04/11

NANCY DREW

THE NEW CASE FILES

Girl Detective®

VAMPIRE SLAYER PART TWO

STEFAN PETRUCHA & SARAH KINNEY • Writers
SHO MURASE • Artist
with 3D CG elements and color by CARLOS JOSE GUZMAN
Based on the series by
CAROLYN KEENE

New York

Let me introduce myself. I'm Nancy Drew. My friends call me Nancy. My enemies call me a lot of other things better left unsaid. See, I'm a detective. Not really. I mean, I don't have a license or anything. I don't carry a gun (not that I would touch one of those even if I could) or a badge. I'm not even old enough to have one. But I am old enough to know when something isn't right, when somebody's getting an unfair deal, or when someone's done something they shouldn't do. And I know how to stop them, catch them, and get them into the hands of the law, where they belong. I take those things seriously and I'm almost never wrong.

"Vampire Slayer" Part Two
STEFAN PETRUCHA & SARAH KINNEY – Writers
SHO MURASE — Artist
with 3D CG elements and color by CARLOS JOSE GUZMAN
BRYAN SENKA – Letterer
CHRIS NELSON & SHELLY STERNER – Production
MICHAEL PETRANEK – Associate Editor
JIM SALICRUP
Editor-in-Chief

ISBN: 978-1-59707-233-5 paperback edition
ISBN: 978-1-59707-234-2 hardcover edition

Copyright © 2011 by Simon & Schuster, Inc. Published by arrangement with Aladdin Paperbacks, an imprint of Simon & Schuster Children's Publishing Division. Nancy Drew is a trademark of Simon & Schuster, Inc. All rights reserved.

Printed in China.
September 2010 by Asia One Printing LTD.
13/F Asia One Tower
8 Fung Yip St., Chaiwan
Hong Kong

Distributed by Macmillan.

First Printing

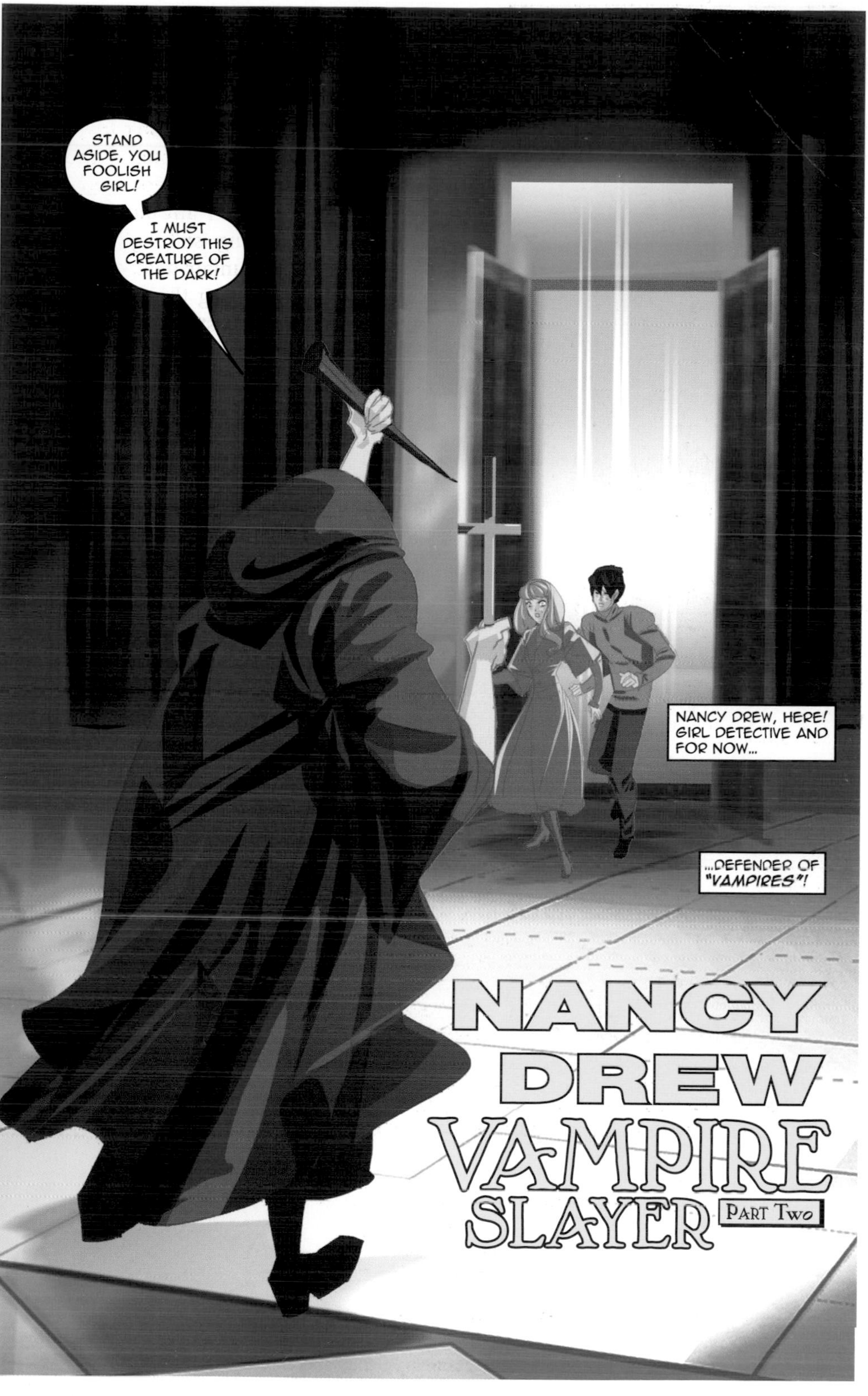
STAND ASIDE, YOU FOOLISH GIRL!
I MUST DESTROY THIS CREATURE OF THE DARK!
NANCY DREW, HERE! GIRL DETECTIVE AND FOR NOW...
...DEFENDER OF "VAMPIRES"!
NANCY DREW
VAMPIRE SLAYER
PART TWO

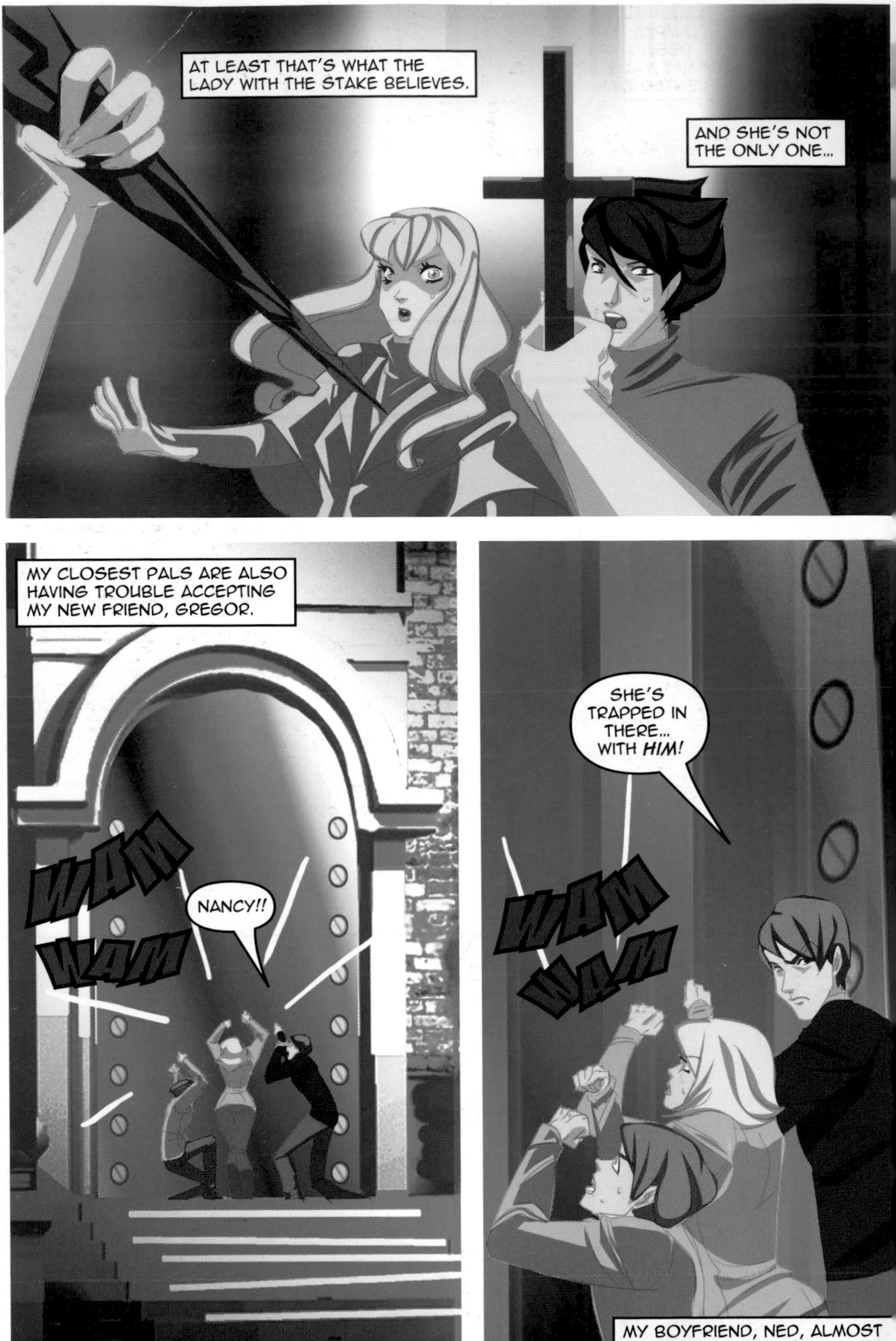
AT LEAST THAT'S WHAT THE LADY WITH THE STAKE BELIEVES.
AND SHE'S NOT THE ONLY ONE...
MY CLOSEST PALS ARE ALSO HAVING TROUBLE ACCEPTING MY NEW FRIEND, GREGOR.
WAM
WAM
NANCY!!
SHE'S TRAPPED IN THERE... WITH *HIM*!
WAM
WAM
MY BOYFRIEND, NED, ALMOST NEVER GETS *JEALOUS*. BUT, *THIS GUY* REALLY SET HIM OFF.

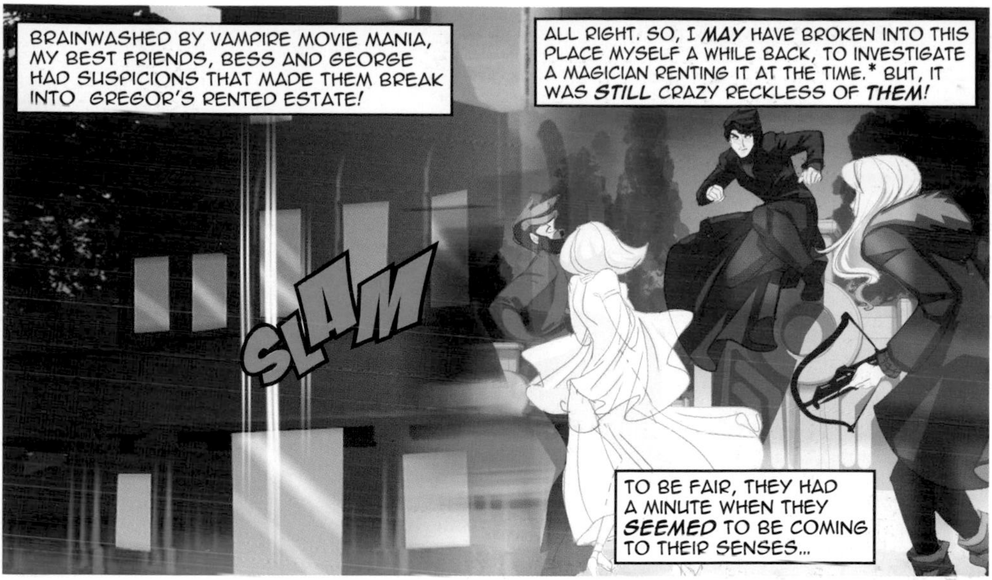
BRAINWASHED BY VAMPIRE MOVIE MANIA, MY BEST FRIENDS, BESS AND GEORGE HAD SUSPICIONS THAT MADE THEM BREAK INTO GREGOR'S RENTED ESTATE!
ALL RIGHT. SO, I *MAY* HAVE BROKEN INTO THIS PLACE MYSELF A WHILE BACK, TO INVESTIGATE A MAGICIAN RENTING IT AT THE TIME.* BUT, IT WAS *STILL* CRAZY RECKLESS OF *THEM!*
SLAM
TO BE FAIR, THEY HAD A MINUTE WHEN THEY *SEEMED* TO BE COMING TO THEIR SENSES...

*SEE NANCY DREW GRAPHIC NOVEL #14 "SLEIGHT OF DAN."

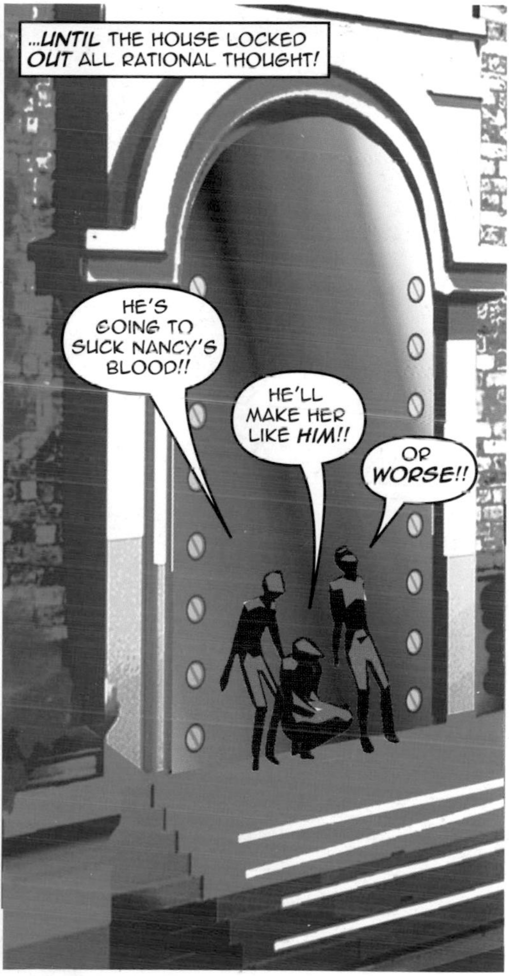
...*UNTIL* THE HOUSE LOCKED *OUT* ALL RATIONAL THOUGHT!
HE'S GOING TO SUCK NANCY'S BLOOD!!
HE'LL MAKE HER LIKE *HIM!!*
OR *WORSE!!*

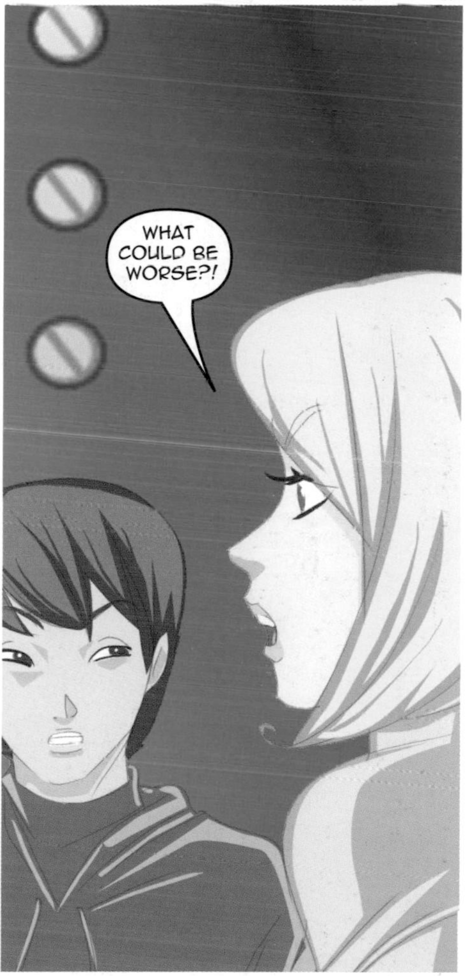
WHAT COULD BE WORSE?!

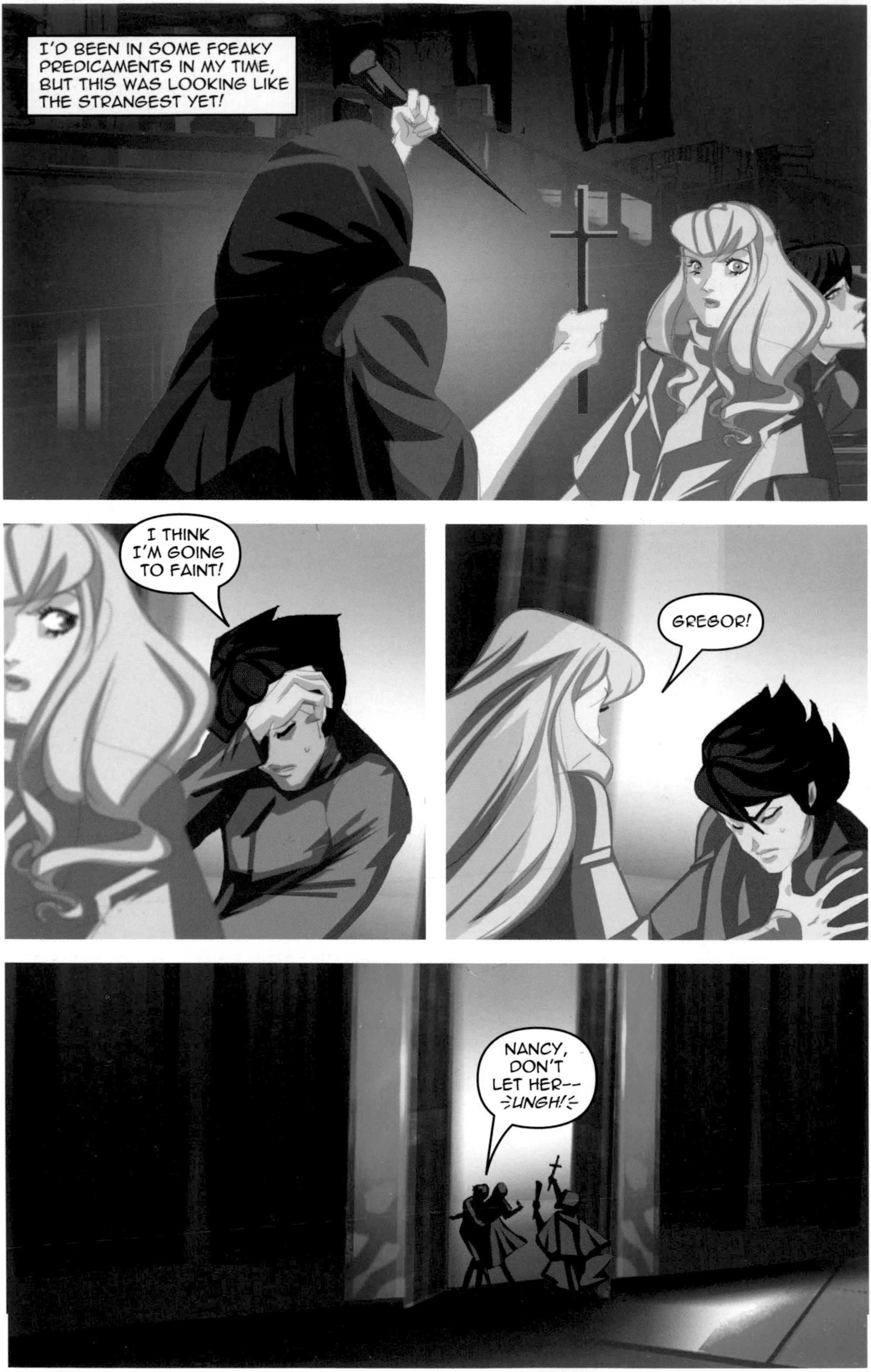
I'D BEEN IN SOME FREAKY PREDICAMENTS IN MY TIME, BUT THIS WAS LOOKING LIKE THE STRANGEST YET!
I THINK I'M GOING TO FAINT!
GREGOR!
NANCY, DON'T LET HER-- UNGH!

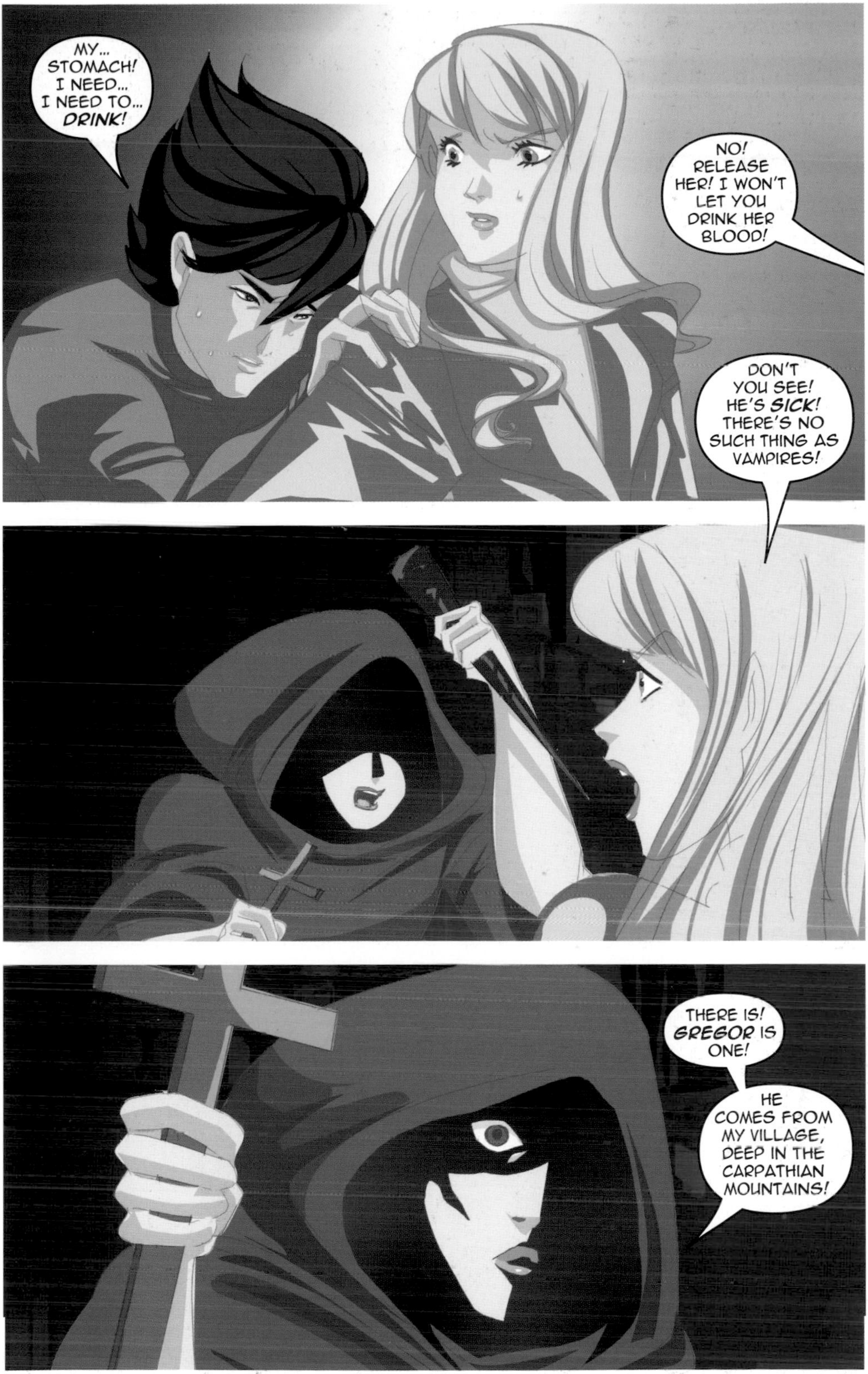
MY... STOMACH! I NEED... I NEED TO... DRINK!
NO! RELEASE HER! I WON'T LET YOU DRINK HER BLOOD!
DON'T YOU SEE! HE'S SICK! THERE'S NO SUCH THING AS VAMPIRES!
THERE IS! GREGOR IS ONE!
HE COMES FROM MY VILLAGE, DEEP IN THE CARPATHIAN MOUNTAINS!

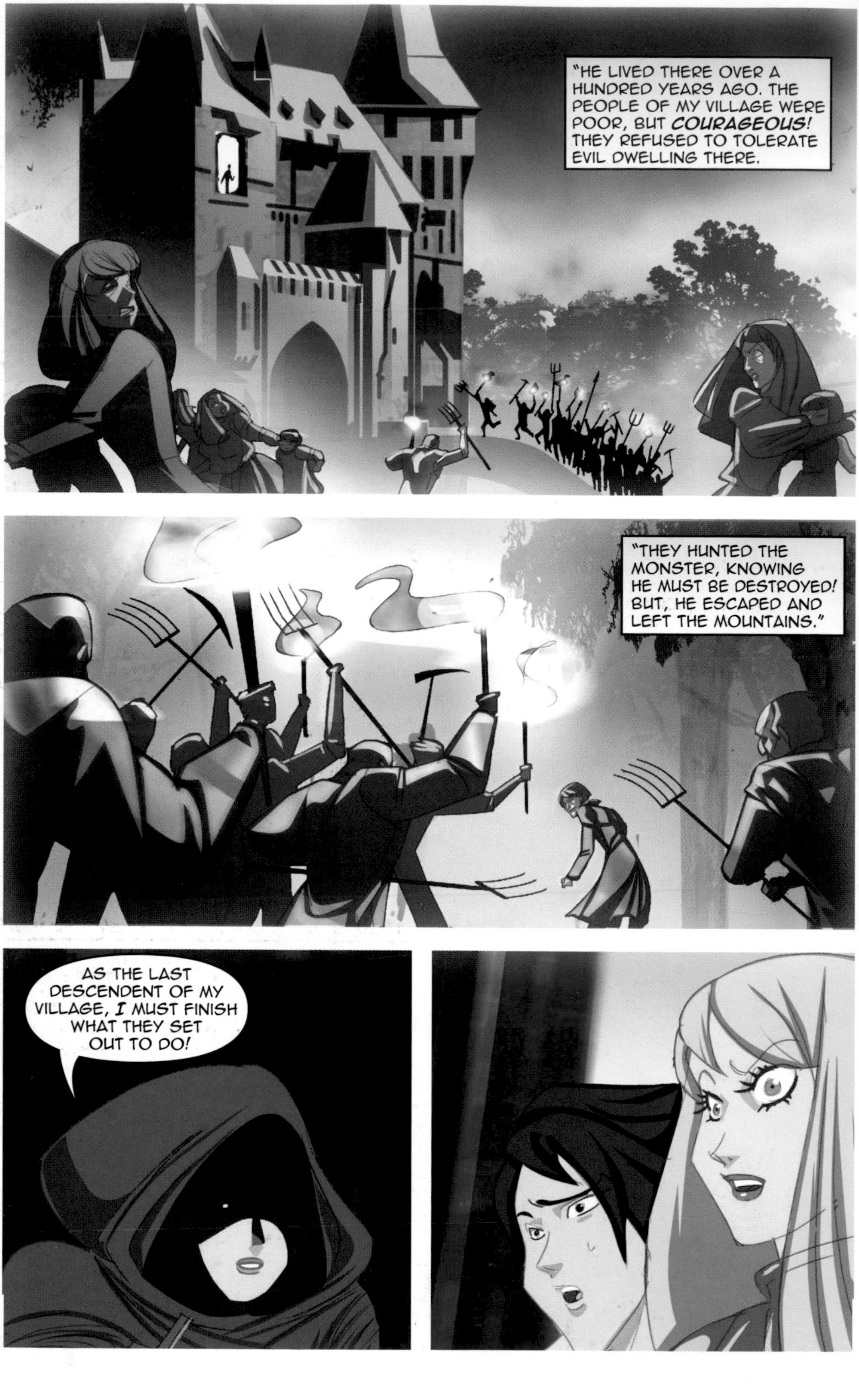
"HE LIVED THERE OVER A HUNDRED YEARS AGO. THE PEOPLE OF MY VILLAGE WERE POOR, BUT COURAGEOUS! THEY REFUSED TO TOLERATE EVIL DWELLING THERE.
"THEY HUNTED THE MONSTER, KNOWING HE MUST BE DESTROYED! BUT, HE ESCAPED AND LEFT THE MOUNTAINS."
AS THE LAST DESCENDENT OF MY VILLAGE, I MUST FINISH WHAT THEY SET OUT TO DO!

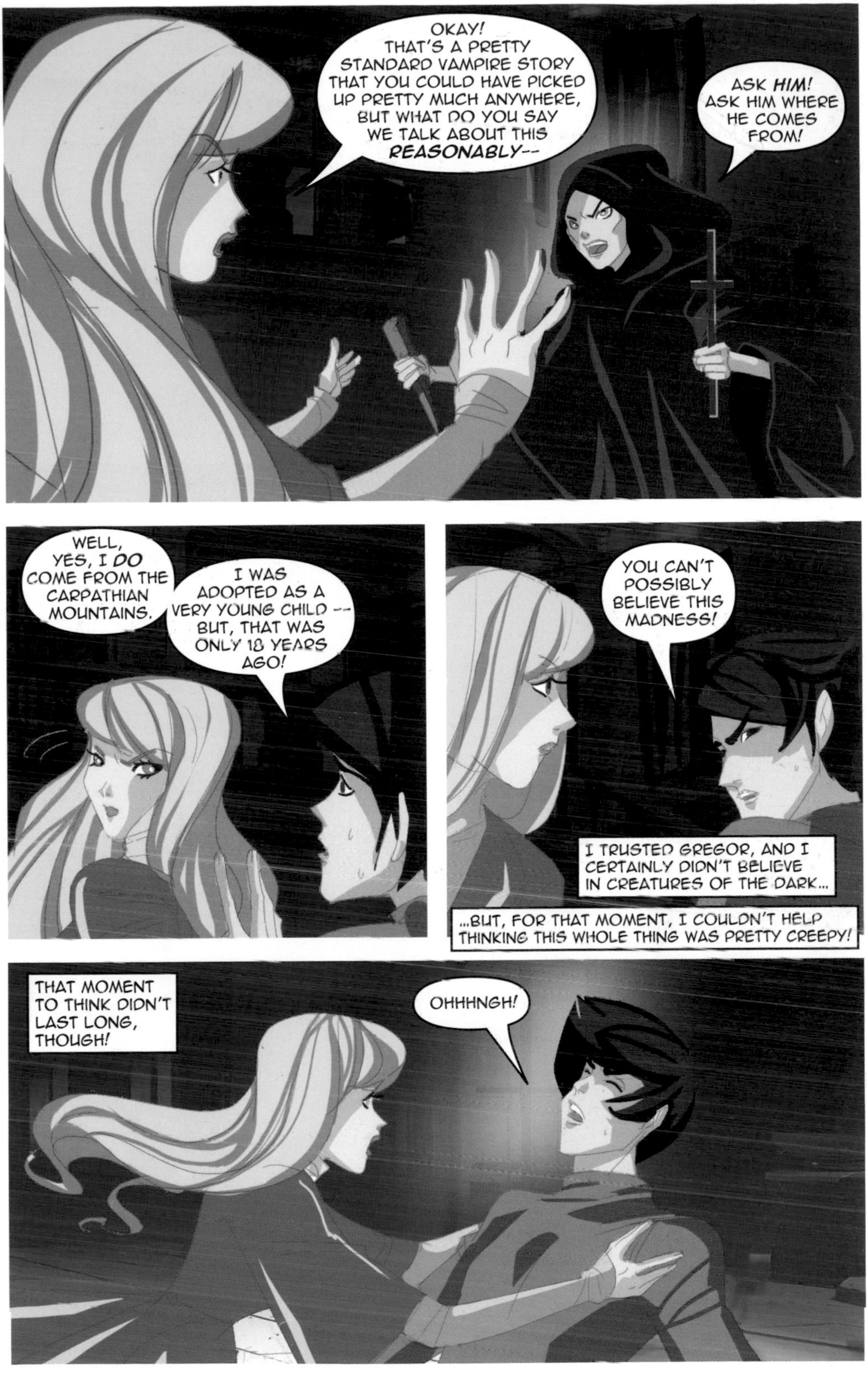
OKAY! THAT'S A PRETTY STANDARD VAMPIRE STORY THAT YOU COULD HAVE PICKED UP PRETTY MUCH ANYWHERE, BUT WHAT DO YOU SAY WE TALK ABOUT THIS *REASONABLY*--
ASK *HIM*! ASK HIM WHERE HE COMES FROM!
WELL, YES, I *DO* COME FROM THE CARPATHIAN MOUNTAINS.
I WAS ADOPTED AS A VERY YOUNG CHILD -- BUT, THAT WAS ONLY 18 YEARS AGO!
YOU CAN'T POSSIBLY BELIEVE THIS MADNESS!
I TRUSTED GREGOR, AND I CERTAINLY DIDN'T BELIEVE IN CREATURES OF THE DARK...
...BUT, FOR THAT MOMENT, I COULDN'T HELP THINKING THIS WHOLE THING WAS PRETTY CREEPY!
THAT MOMENT TO THINK DIDN'T LAST LONG, THOUGH!
OHHHNGH!

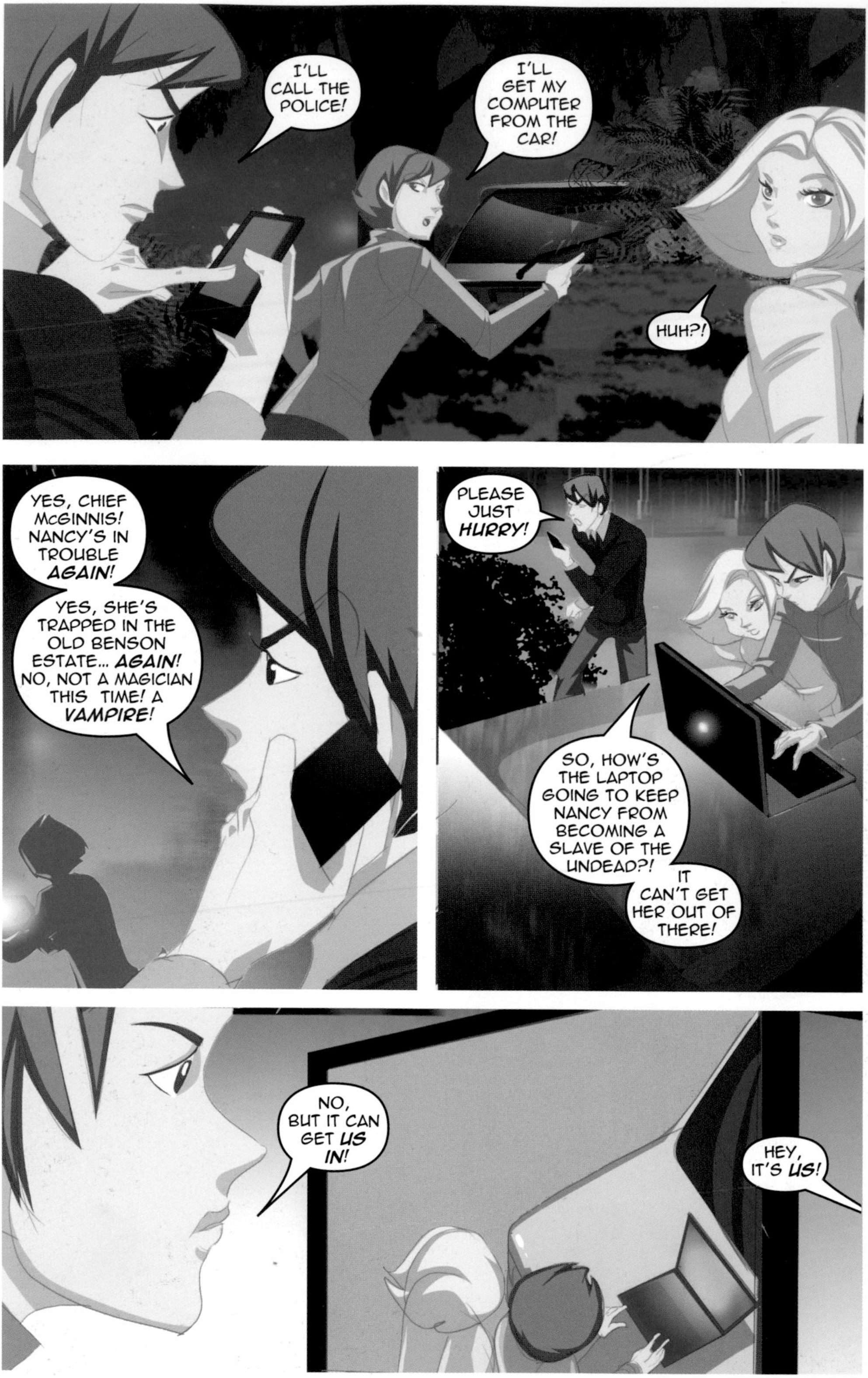

I'LL CALL THE POLICE!
I'LL GET MY COMPUTER FROM THE CAR!
HUH?!
YES, CHIEF McGINNIS! NANCY'S IN TROUBLE **AGAIN**!
YES, SHE'S TRAPPED IN THE OLD BENSON ESTATE... **AGAIN**! NO, NOT A MAGICIAN THIS TIME! A **VAMPIRE**!
PLEASE JUST **HURRY**!
SO, HOW'S THE LAPTOP GOING TO KEEP NANCY FROM BECOMING A SLAVE OF THE UNDEAD?!
IT CAN'T GET HER OUT OF THERE!
NO, BUT IT CAN GET **US IN**!
HEY, IT'S **US**!

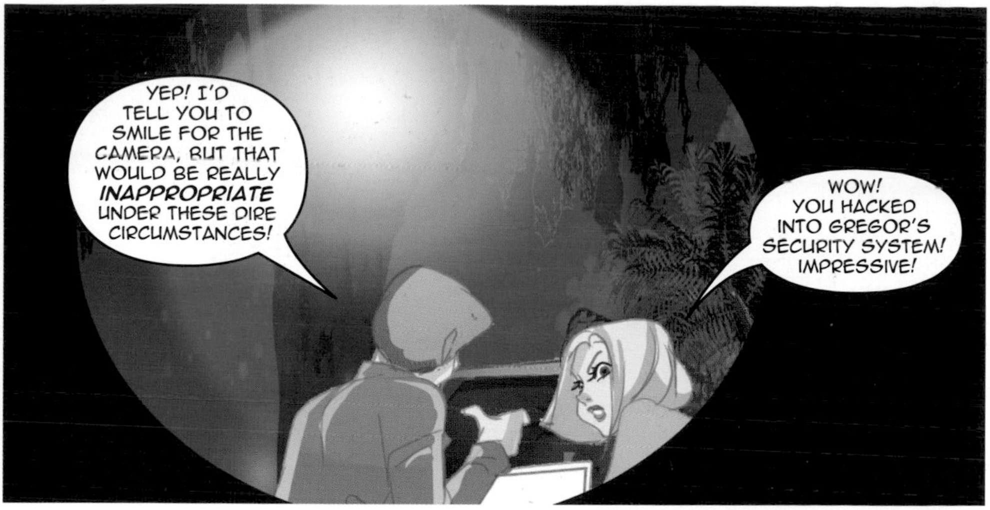
YEP! I'D TELL YOU TO SMILE FOR THE CAMERA, BUT THAT WOULD BE REALLY INAPPROPRIATE UNDER THESE DIRE CIRCUMSTANCES!
WOW! YOU HACKED INTO GREGOR'S SECURITY SYSTEM! IMPRESSIVE!

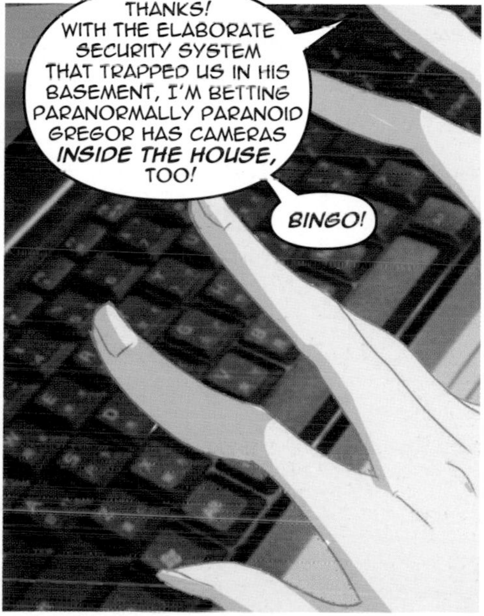
THANKS! WITH THE ELABORATE SECURITY SYSTEM THAT TRAPPED US IN HIS BASEMENT, I'M BETTING PARANORMALLY PARANOID GREGOR HAS CAMERAS INSIDE THE HOUSE, TOO!
BINGO!

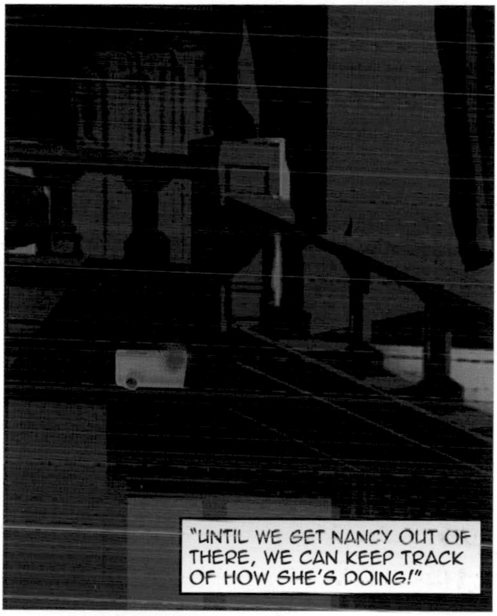
"UNTIL WE GET NANCY OUT OF THERE, WE CAN KEEP TRACK OF HOW SHE'S DOING!"

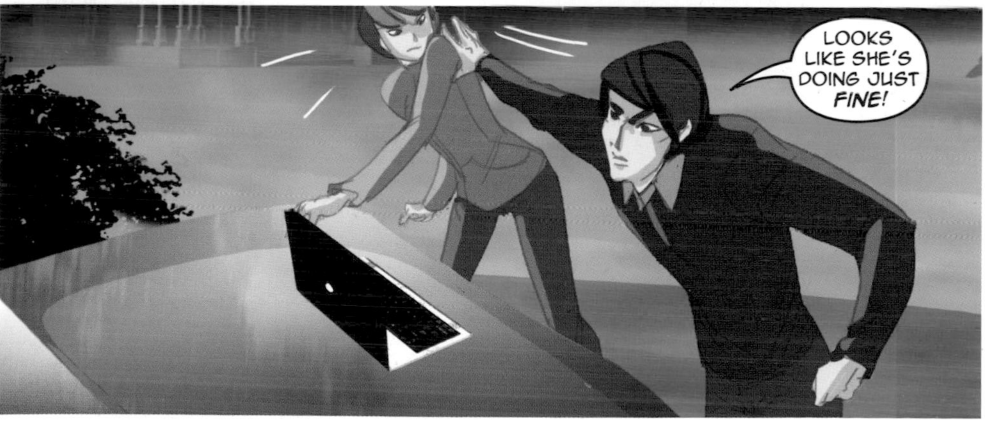
LOOKS LIKE SHE'S DOING JUST FINE!

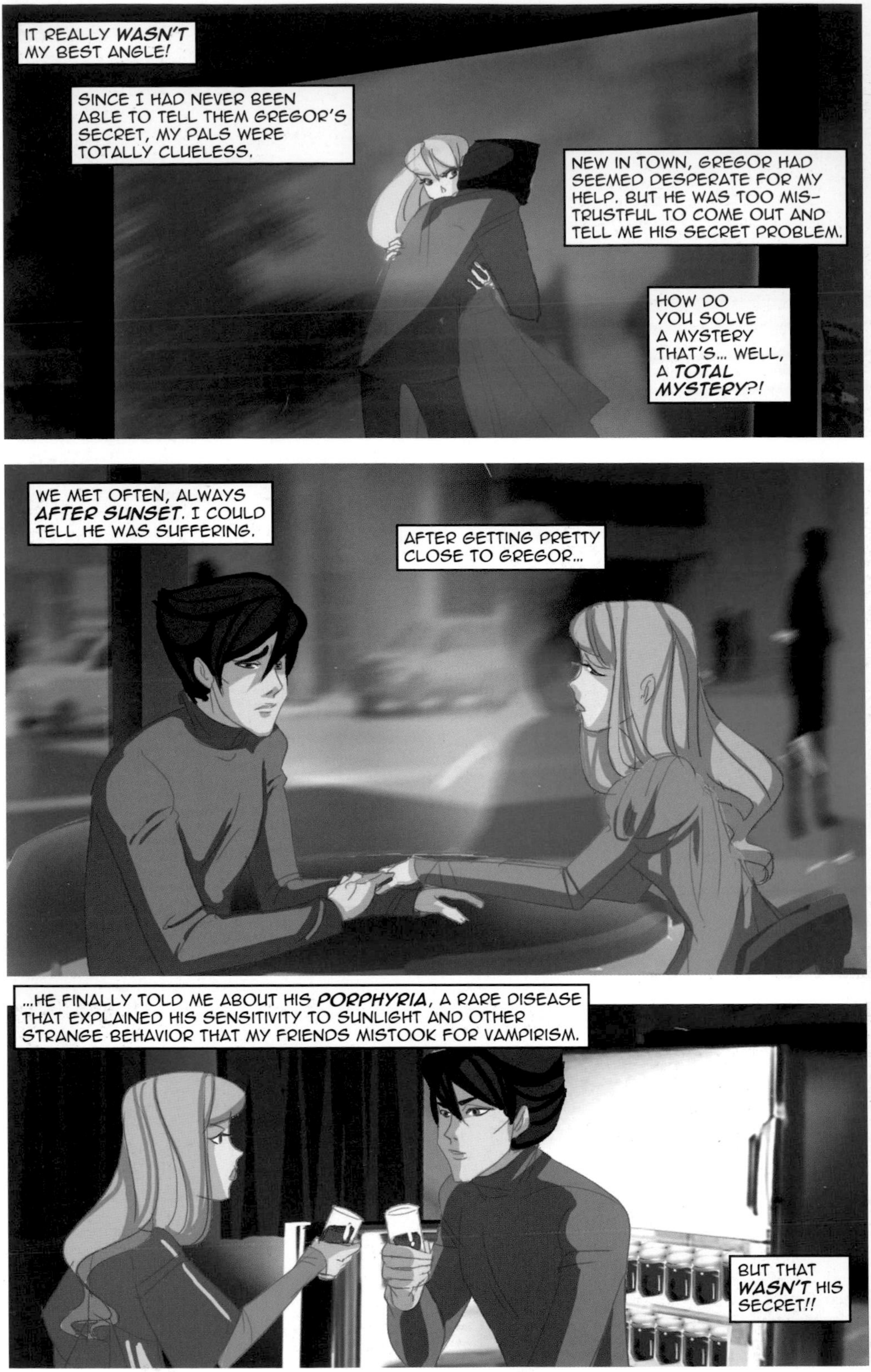
IT REALLY WASN'T MY BEST ANGLE!
SINCE I HAD NEVER BEEN ABLE TO TELL THEM GREGOR'S SECRET, MY PALS WERE TOTALLY CLUELESS.
NEW IN TOWN, GREGOR HAD SEEMED DESPERATE FOR MY HELP. BUT HE WAS TOO MIS-TRUSTFUL TO COME OUT AND TELL ME HIS SECRET PROBLEM.
HOW DO YOU SOLVE A MYSTERY THAT'S... WELL, A TOTAL MYSTERY?!
WE MET OFTEN, ALWAYS AFTER SUNSET. I COULD TELL HE WAS SUFFERING.
AFTER GETTING PRETTY CLOSE TO GREGOR...
...HE FINALLY TOLD ME ABOUT HIS PORPHYRIA, A RARE DISEASE THAT EXPLAINED HIS SENSITIVITY TO SUNLIGHT AND OTHER STRANGE BEHAVIOR THAT MY FRIENDS MISTOOK FOR VAMPIRISM.
BUT THAT WASN'T HIS SECRET!!

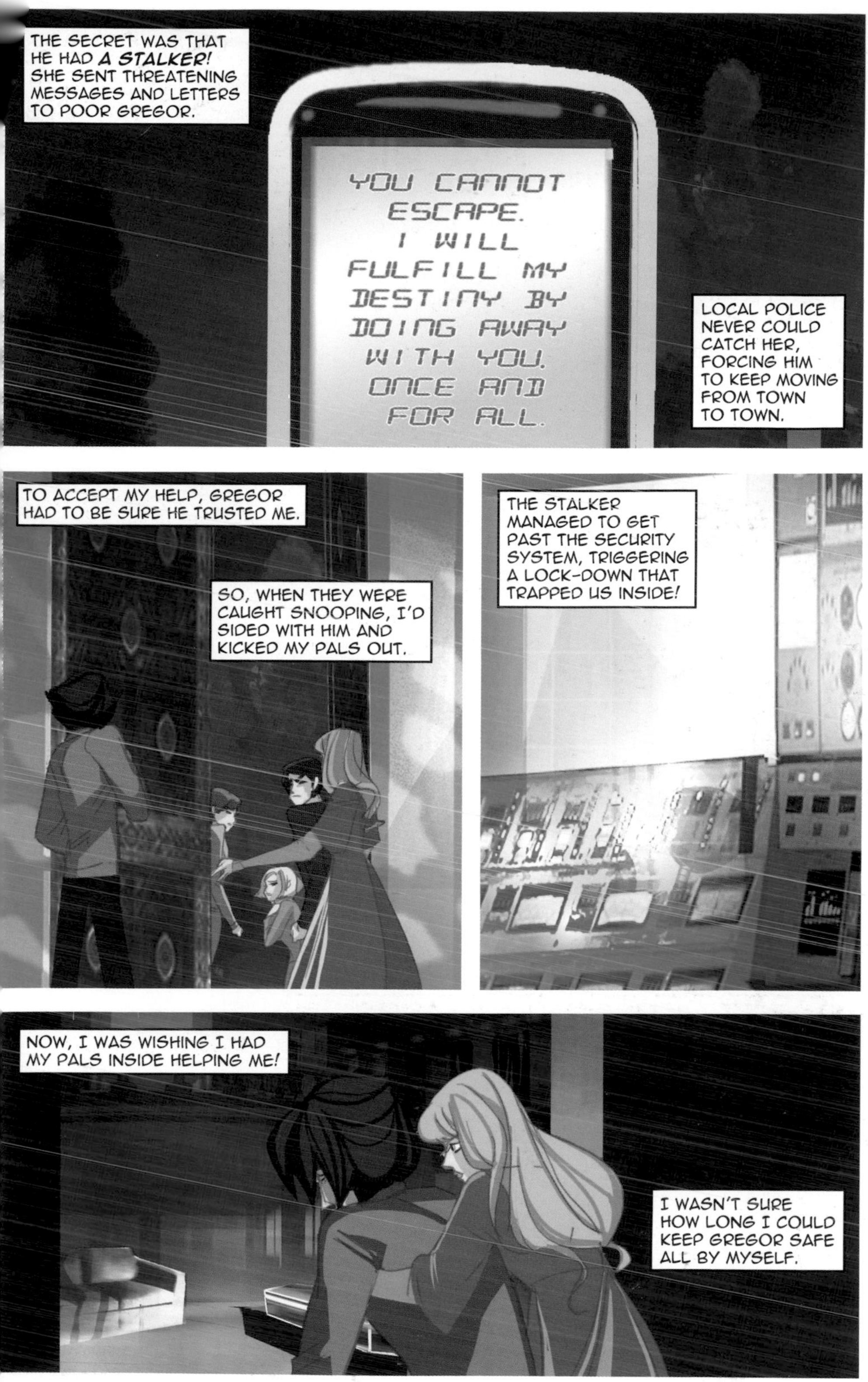

THE SECRET WAS THAT HE HAD A STALKER! SHE SENT THREATENING MESSAGES AND LETTERS TO POOR GREGOR.
YOU CANNOT ESCAPE. I WILL FULFILL MY DESTINY BY DOING AWAY WITH YOU. ONCE AND FOR ALL.
LOCAL POLICE NEVER COULD CATCH HER, FORCING HIM TO KEEP MOVING FROM TOWN TO TOWN.
TO ACCEPT MY HELP, GREGOR HAD TO BE SURE HE TRUSTED ME.
SO, WHEN THEY WERE CAUGHT SNOOPING, I'D SIDED WITH HIM AND KICKED MY PALS OUT.
THE STALKER MANAGED TO GET PAST THE SECURITY SYSTEM, TRIGGERING A LOCK-DOWN THAT TRAPPED US INSIDE!
NOW, I WAS WISHING I HAD MY PALS INSIDE HELPING ME!
I WASN'T SURE HOW LONG I COULD KEEP GREGOR SAFE ALL BY MYSELF.

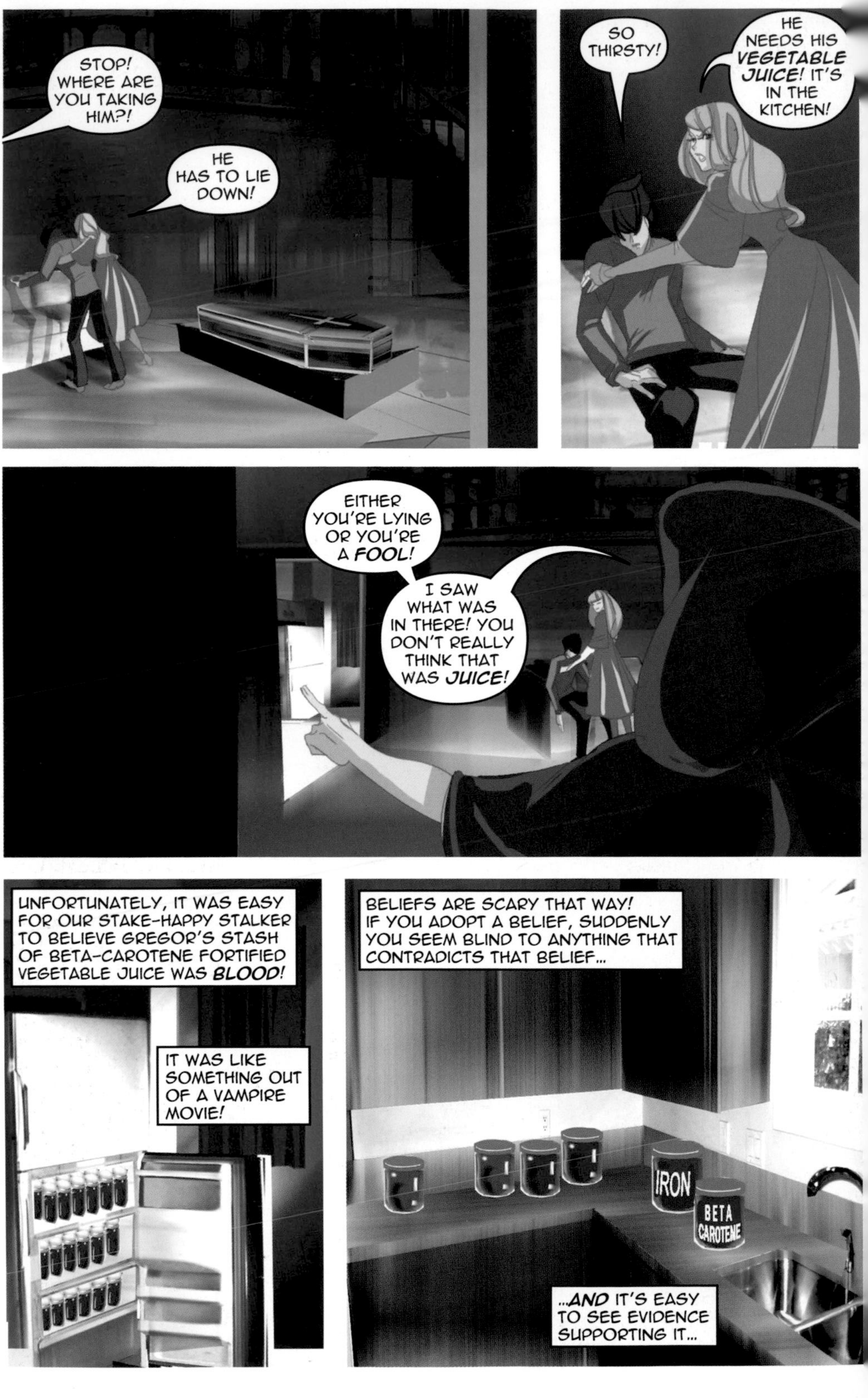

STOP! WHERE ARE YOU TAKING HIM?!
HE HAS TO LIE DOWN!
SO THIRSTY!
HE NEEDS HIS VEGETABLE JUICE! IT'S IN THE KITCHEN!
EITHER YOU'RE LYING OR YOU'RE A FOOL!
I SAW WHAT WAS IN THERE! YOU DON'T REALLY THINK THAT WAS JUICE!
UNFORTUNATELY, IT WAS EASY FOR OUR STAKE-HAPPY STALKER TO BELIEVE GREGOR'S STASH OF BETA-CAROTENE FORTIFIED VEGETABLE JUICE WAS BLOOD!
IT WAS LIKE SOMETHING OUT OF A VAMPIRE MOVIE!
BELIEFS ARE SCARY THAT WAY! IF YOU ADOPT A BELIEF, SUDDENLY YOU SEEM BLIND TO ANYTHING THAT CONTRADICTS THAT BELIEF...
IRON
BETA CAROTENE
...AND IT'S EASY TO SEE EVIDENCE SUPPORTING IT...

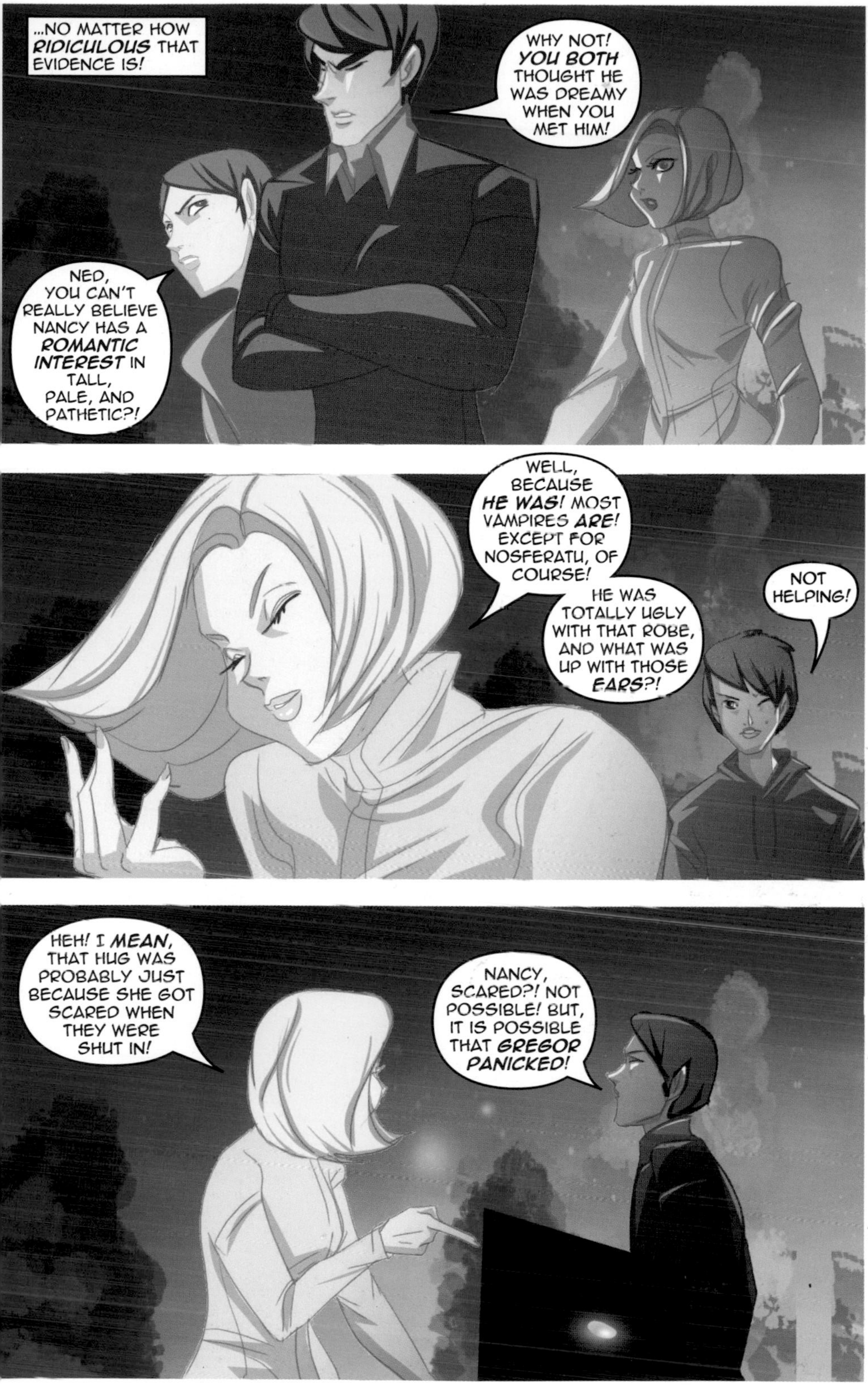
...NO MATTER HOW RIDICULOUS THAT EVIDENCE IS!
WHY NOT! YOU BOTH THOUGHT HE WAS DREAMY WHEN YOU MET HIM!
NED, YOU CAN'T REALLY BELIEVE NANCY HAS A ROMANTIC INTEREST IN TALL, PALE, AND PATHETIC?!
WELL, BECAUSE HE WAS! MOST VAMPIRES ARE! EXCEPT FOR NOSFERATU, OF COURSE!
HE WAS TOTALLY UGLY WITH THAT ROBE, AND WHAT WAS UP WITH THOSE EARS?!
NOT HELPING!
HEH! I MEAN, THAT HUG WAS PROBABLY JUST BECAUSE SHE GOT SCARED WHEN THEY WERE SHUT IN!
NANCY, SCARED?! NOT POSSIBLE! BUT, IT IS POSSIBLE THAT GREGOR PANICKED!

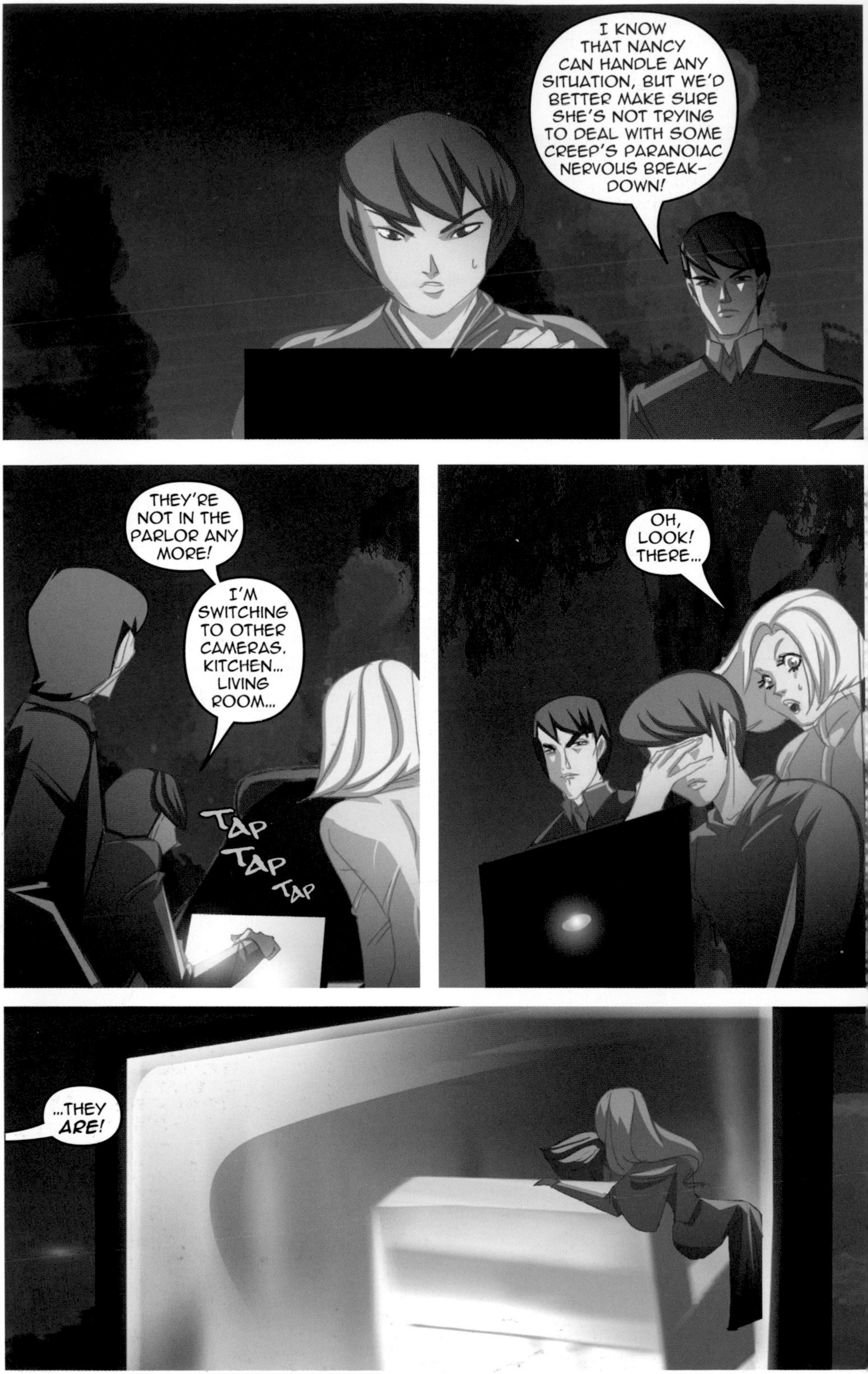
I KNOW THAT NANCY CAN HANDLE ANY SITUATION, BUT WE'D BETTER MAKE SURE SHE'S NOT TRYING TO DEAL WITH SOME CREEP'S PARANOIAC NERVOUS BREAK-DOWN!
THEY'RE NOT IN THE PARLOR ANY MORE!
I'M SWITCHING TO OTHER CAMERAS. KITCHEN... LIVING ROOM...
TAP TAP TAP
OH, LOOK! THERE...
...THEY ARE!

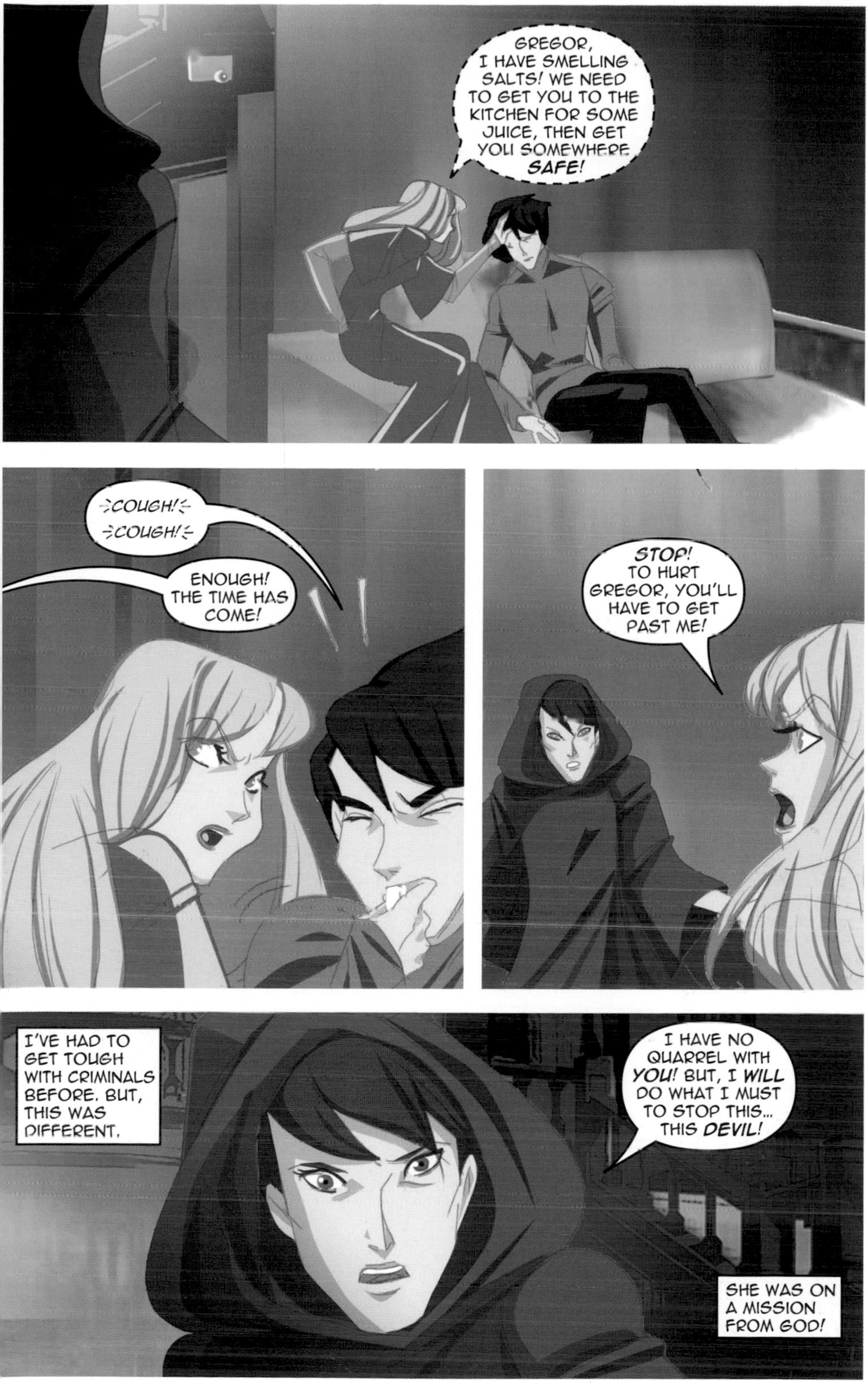
GREGOR, I HAVE SMELLING SALTS! WE NEED TO GET YOU TO THE KITCHEN FOR SOME JUICE, THEN GET YOU SOMEWHERE *SAFE!*
COUGH!
COUGH!
ENOUGH! THE TIME HAS COME!
STOP! TO HURT GREGOR, YOU'LL HAVE TO GET PAST ME!
I'VE HAD TO GET TOUGH WITH CRIMINALS BEFORE. BUT, THIS WAS DIFFERENT.
I HAVE NO QUARREL WITH *YOU!* BUT, I *WILL* DO WHAT I MUST TO STOP THIS... THIS *DEVIL!*
SHE WAS ON A MISSION FROM GOD!

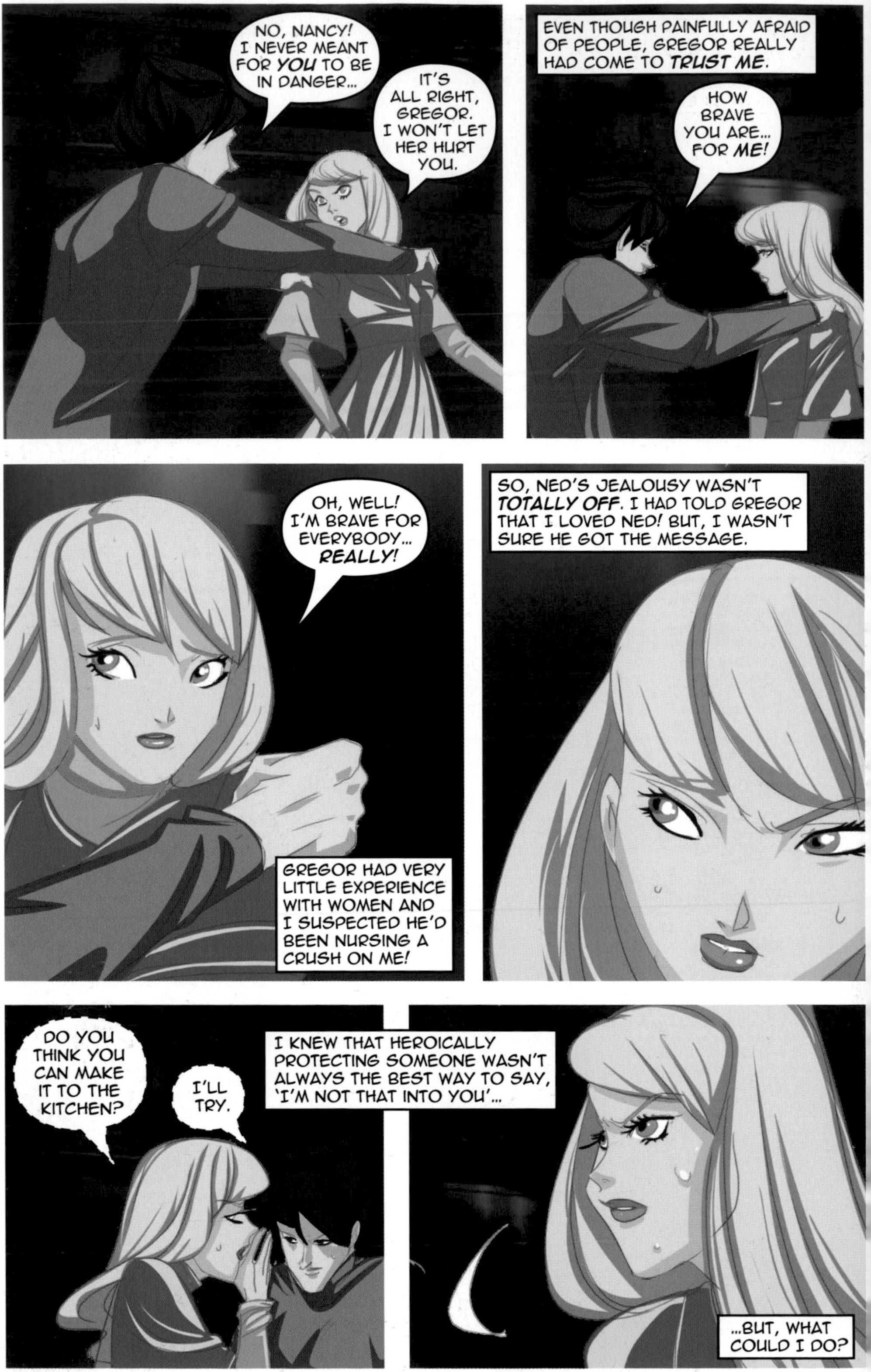
NO, NANCY! I NEVER MEANT FOR YOU TO BE IN DANGER...
IT'S ALL RIGHT, GREGOR. I WON'T LET HER HURT YOU.
EVEN THOUGH PAINFULLY AFRAID OF PEOPLE, GREGOR REALLY HAD COME TO TRUST ME.
HOW BRAVE YOU ARE... FOR ME!
OH, WELL! I'M BRAVE FOR EVERYBODY... REALLY!
GREGOR HAD VERY LITTLE EXPERIENCE WITH WOMEN AND I SUSPECTED HE'D BEEN NURSING A CRUSH ON ME!
SO, NED'S JEALOUSY WASN'T TOTALLY OFF. I HAD TOLD GREGOR THAT I LOVED NED! BUT, I WASN'T SURE HE GOT THE MESSAGE.
DO YOU THINK YOU CAN MAKE IT TO THE KITCHEN?
I'LL TRY.
I KNEW THAT HEROICALLY PROTECTING SOMEONE WASN'T ALWAYS THE BEST WAY TO SAY, 'I'M NOT THAT INTO YOU'...
...BUT, WHAT COULD I DO?

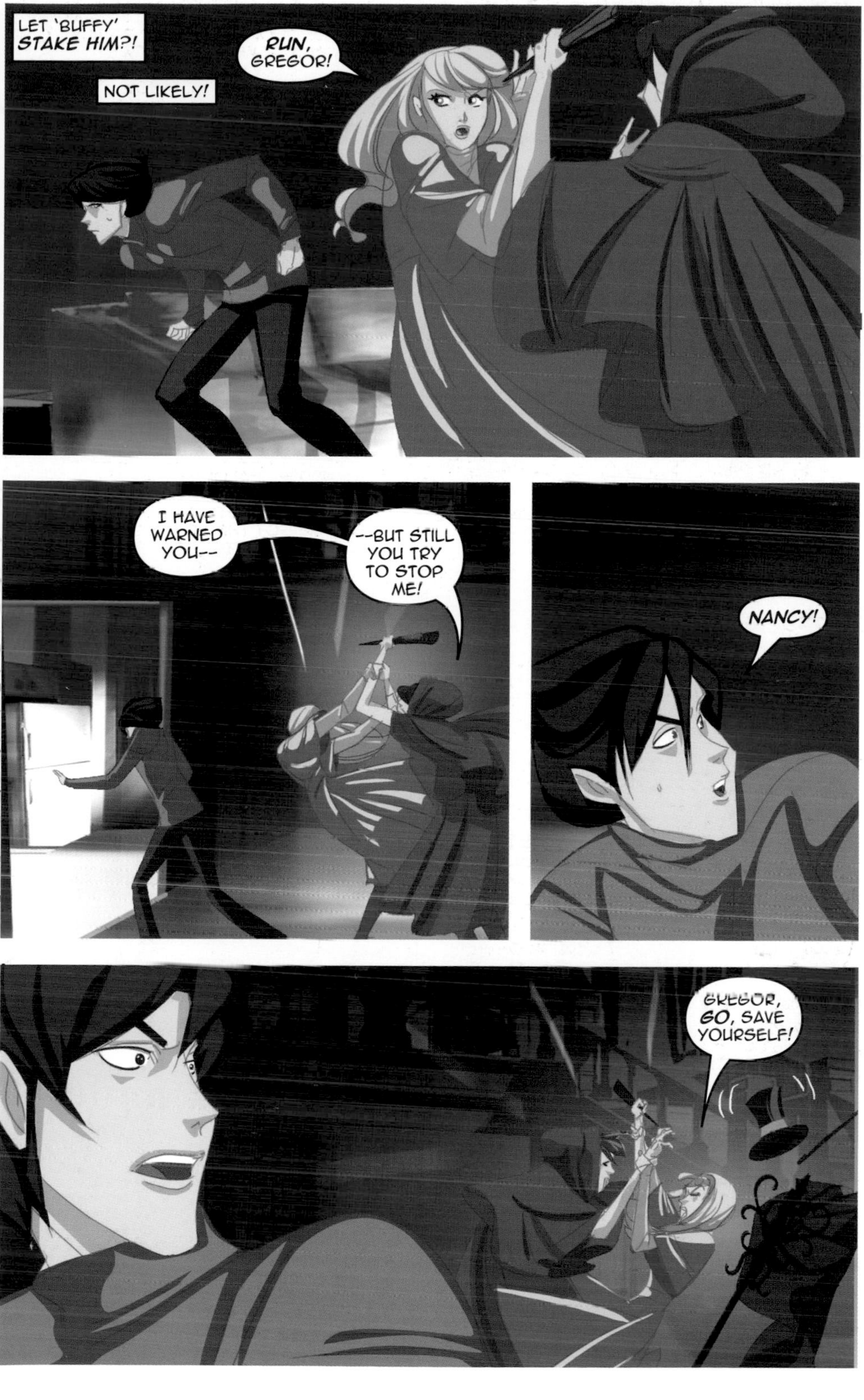
LET 'BUFFY' STAKE HIM?!
NOT LIKELY!
RUN, GREGOR!
I HAVE WARNED YOU--
--BUT STILL YOU TRY TO STOP ME!
NANCY!
GREGOR, GO, SAVE YOURSELF!

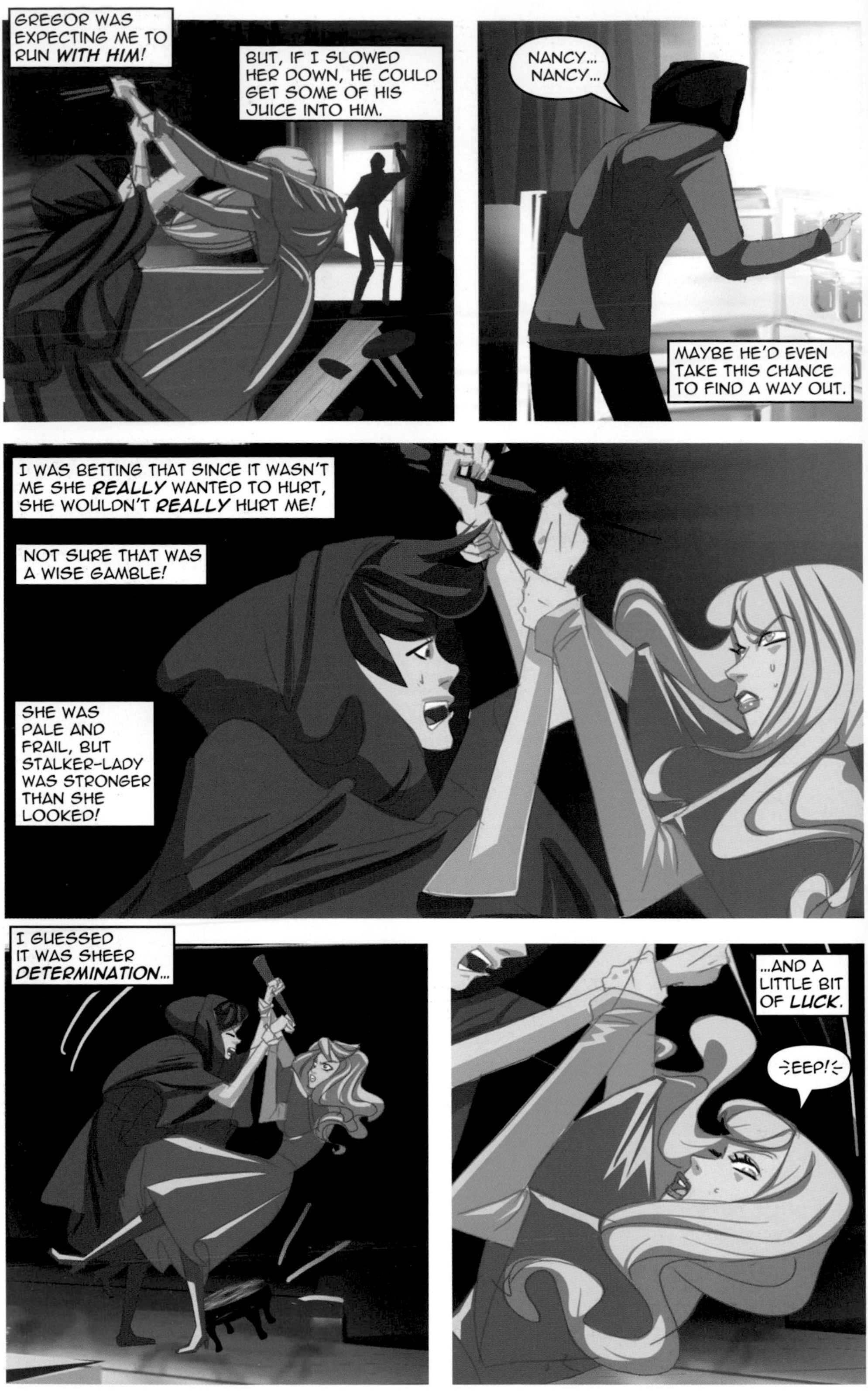
GREGOR WAS EXPECTING ME TO RUN WITH HIM!
BUT, IF I SLOWED HER DOWN, HE COULD GET SOME OF HIS JUICE INTO HIM.
NANCY... NANCY...
MAYBE HE'D EVEN TAKE THIS CHANCE TO FIND A WAY OUT.
I WAS BETTING THAT SINCE IT WASN'T ME SHE REALLY WANTED TO HURT, SHE WOULDN'T REALLY HURT ME!
NOT SURE THAT WAS A WISE GAMBLE!
SHE WAS PALE AND FRAIL, BUT STALKER-LADY WAS STRONGER THAN SHE LOOKED!
I GUESSED IT WAS SHEER DETERMINATION...
...AND A LITTLE BIT OF LUCK.
EEP!

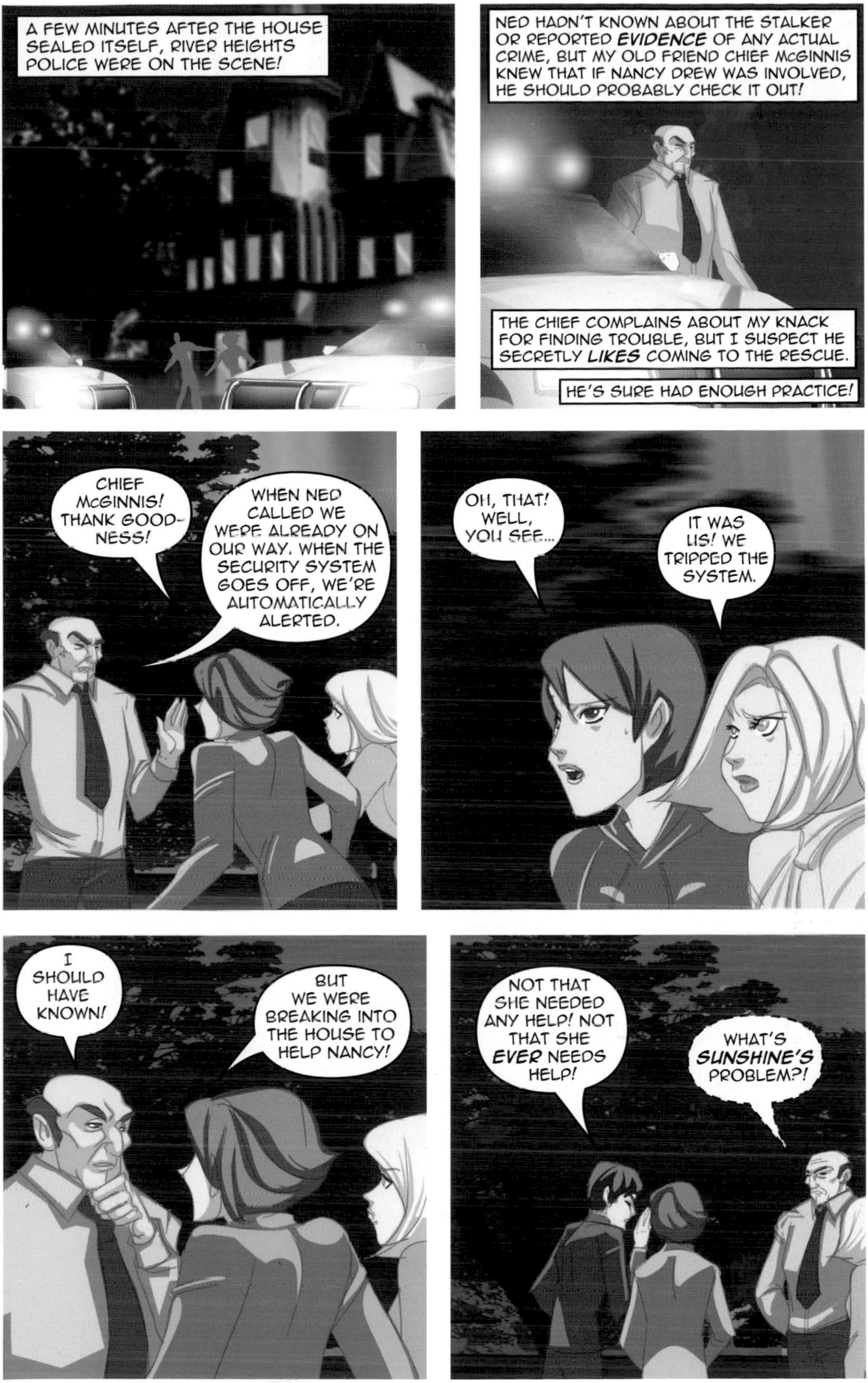
A FEW MINUTES AFTER THE HOUSE SEALED ITSELF, RIVER HEIGHTS POLICE WERE ON THE SCENE!
NED HADN'T KNOWN ABOUT THE STALKER OR REPORTED *EVIDENCE* OF ANY ACTUAL CRIME, BUT MY OLD FRIEND CHIEF McGINNIS KNEW THAT IF NANCY DREW WAS INVOLVED, HE SHOULD PROBABLY CHECK IT OUT!
THE CHIEF COMPLAINS ABOUT MY KNACK FOR FINDING TROUBLE, BUT I SUSPECT HE SECRETLY *LIKES* COMING TO THE RESCUE.
HE'S SURE HAD ENOUGH PRACTICE!
CHIEF McGINNIS! THANK GOODNESS!
WHEN NED CALLED WE WERE ALREADY ON OUR WAY. WHEN THE SECURITY SYSTEM GOES OFF, WE'RE AUTOMATICALLY ALERTED.
OH, THAT! WELL, YOU SEE...
IT WAS US! WE TRIPPED THE SYSTEM.
I SHOULD HAVE KNOWN!
BUT WE WERE BREAKING INTO THE HOUSE TO HELP NANCY!
NOT THAT SHE NEEDED ANY HELP! NOT THAT SHE *EVER* NEEDS HELP!
WHAT'S *SUNSHINE'S* PROBLEM?!

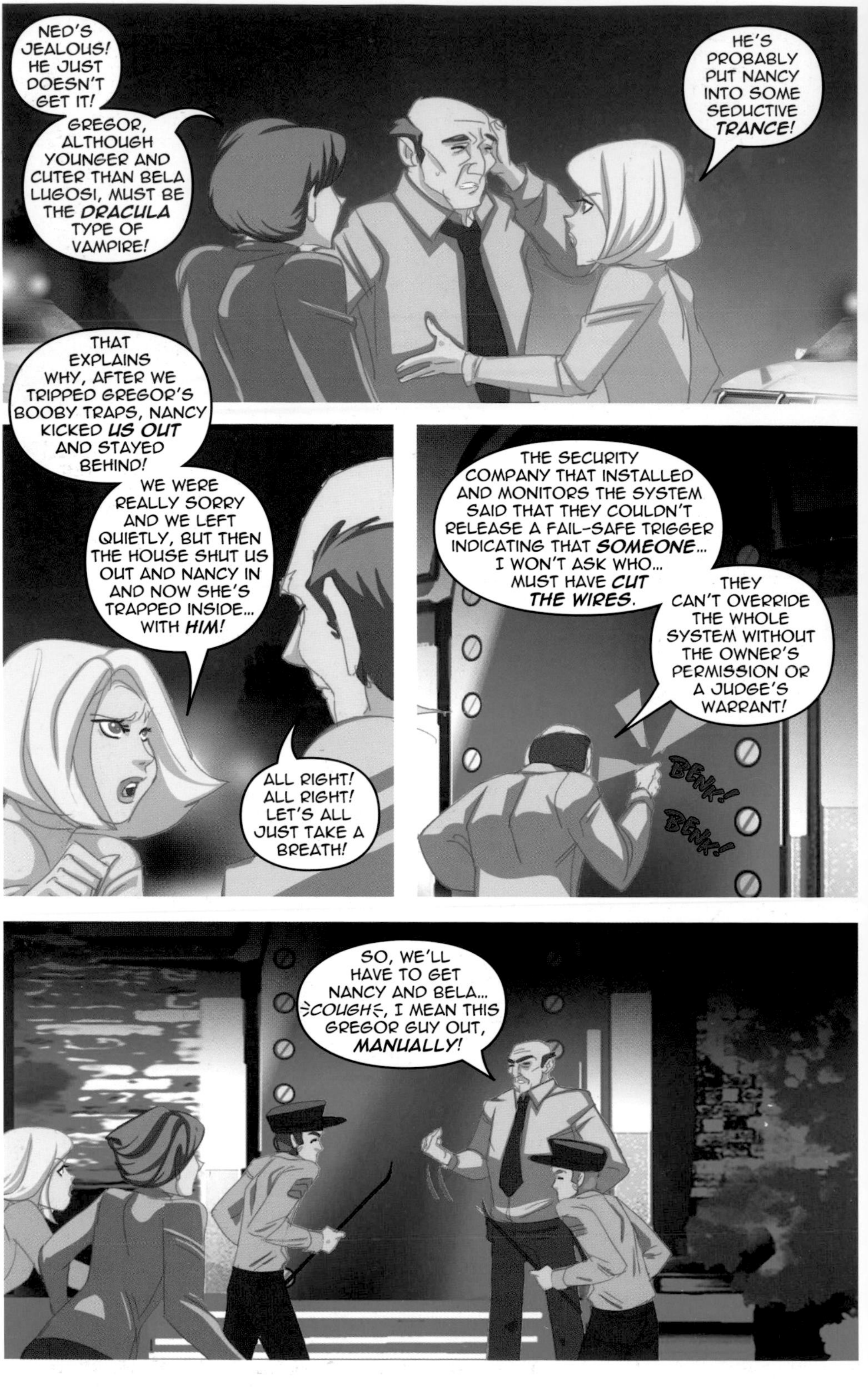

NED'S JEALOUS! HE JUST DOESN'T GET IT!
GREGOR, ALTHOUGH YOUNGER AND CUTER THAN BELA LUGOSI, MUST BE THE *DRACULA* TYPE OF VAMPIRE!
HE'S PROBABLY PUT NANCY INTO SOME SEDUCTIVE *TRANCE!*
THAT EXPLAINS WHY, AFTER WE TRIPPED GREGOR'S BOOBY TRAPS, NANCY KICKED *US OUT* AND STAYED BEHIND!
WE WERE REALLY SORRY AND WE LEFT QUIETLY, BUT THEN THE HOUSE SHUT US OUT AND NANCY IN AND NOW SHE'S TRAPPED INSIDE... WITH *HIM!*
ALL RIGHT! ALL RIGHT! LET'S ALL JUST TAKE A BREATH!
THE SECURITY COMPANY THAT INSTALLED AND MONITORS THE SYSTEM SAID THAT THEY COULDN'T RELEASE A FAIL-SAFE TRIGGER INDICATING THAT *SOMEONE*... I WON'T ASK WHO... MUST HAVE *CUT THE WIRES*.
THEY CAN'T OVERRIDE THE WHOLE SYSTEM WITHOUT THE OWNER'S PERMISSION OR A JUDGE'S WARRANT!
BENK!
BENK!
SO, WE'LL HAVE TO GET NANCY AND BELA... *COUGH*, I MEAN THIS GREGOR GUY OUT, ***MANUALLY!***

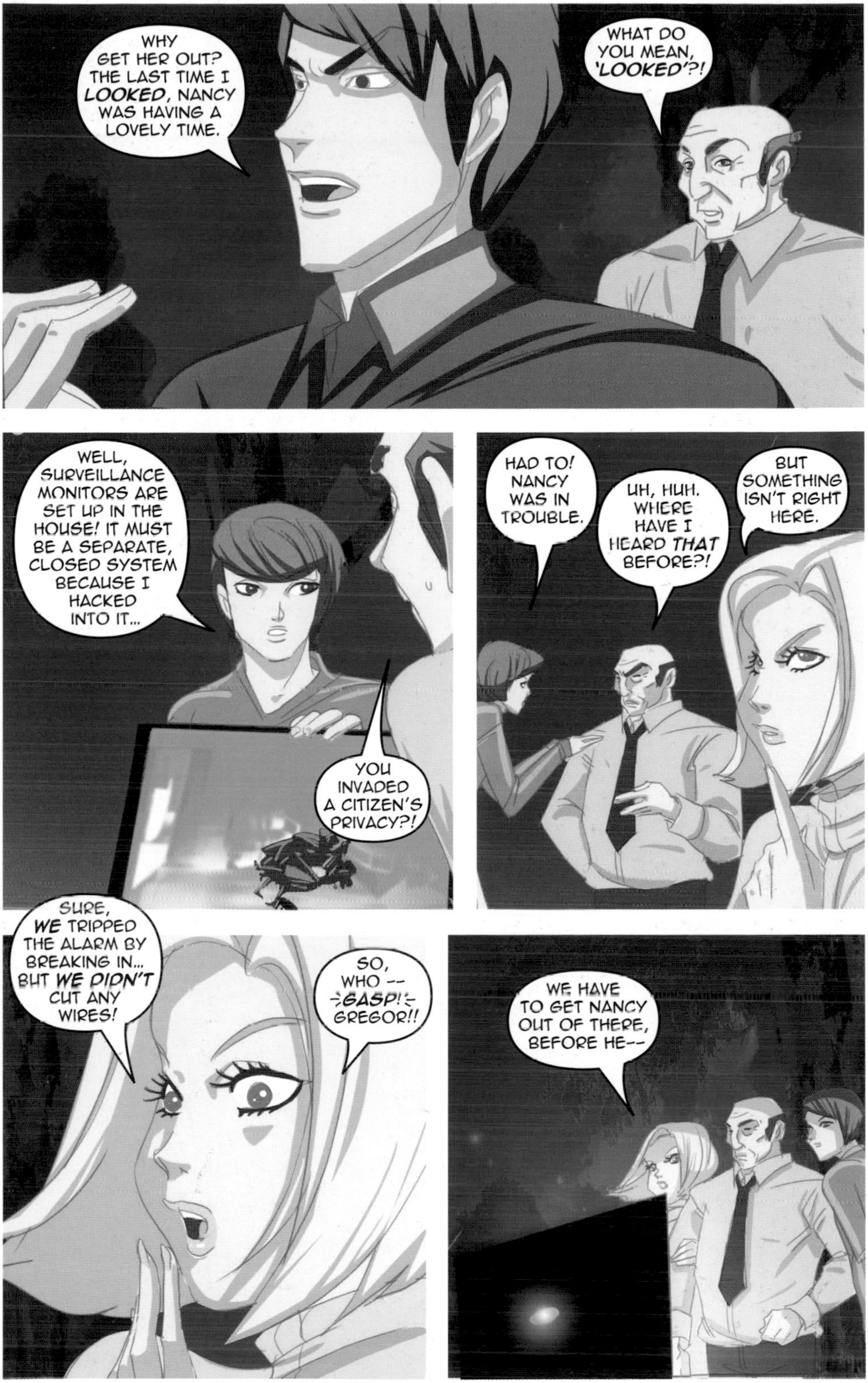
WHY GET HER OUT? THE LAST TIME I *LOOKED*, NANCY WAS HAVING A LOVELY TIME.
WHAT DO YOU MEAN, *'LOOKED'*?!
WELL, SURVEILLANCE MONITORS ARE SET UP IN THE HOUSE! IT MUST BE A SEPARATE, CLOSED SYSTEM BECAUSE I HACKED INTO IT...
YOU INVADED A CITIZEN'S PRIVACY?!
HAD TO! NANCY WAS IN TROUBLE.
UH, HUH. WHERE HAVE I HEARD *THAT* BEFORE?!
BUT SOMETHING ISN'T RIGHT HERE.
SURE, *WE* TRIPPED THE ALARM BY BREAKING IN... BUT *WE DIDN'T* CUT ANY WIRES!
SO, WHO -- *GASP!* GREGOR!!
WE HAVE TO GET NANCY OUT OF THERE, BEFORE HE--

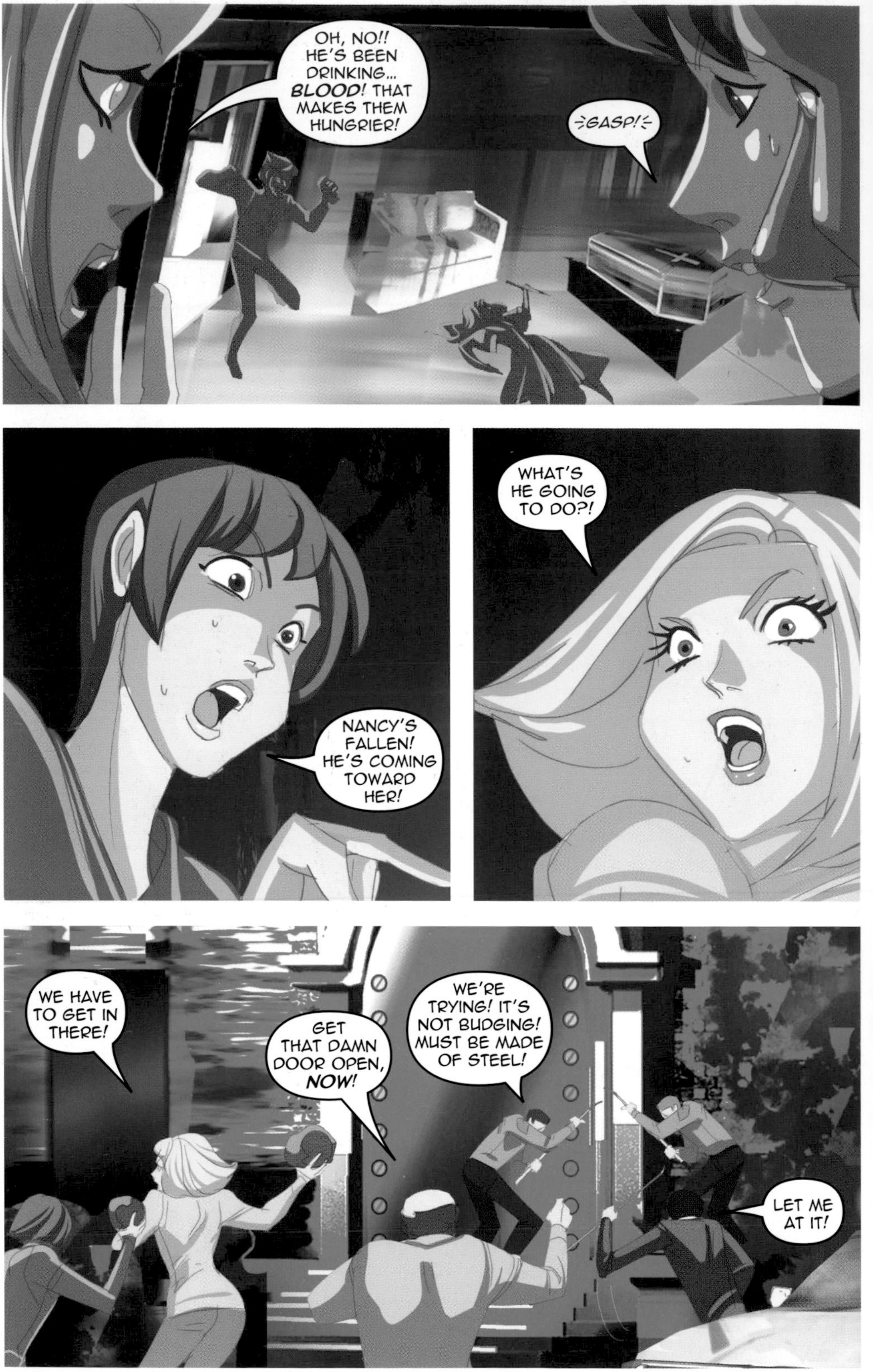
OH, NO!! HE'S BEEN DRINKING... BLOOD! THAT MAKES THEM HUNGRIER!
GASP!
NANCY'S FALLEN! HE'S COMING TOWARD HER!
WHAT'S HE GOING TO DO?!
WE HAVE TO GET IN THERE!
GET THAT DAMN DOOR OPEN, NOW!
WE'RE TRYING! IT'S NOT BUDGING! MUST BE MADE OF STEEL!
LET ME AT IT!

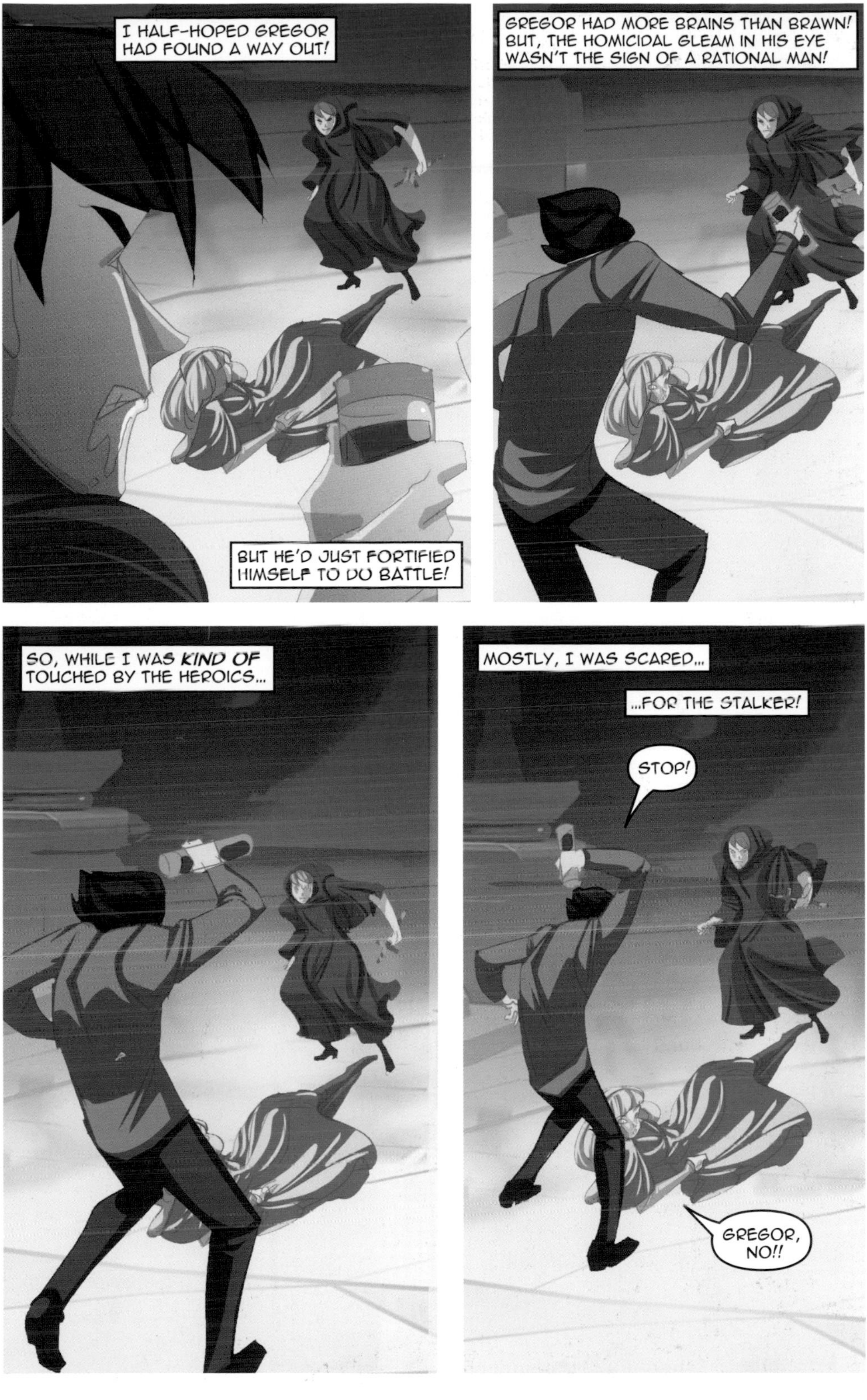
I HALF-HOPED GREGOR HAD FOUND A WAY OUT!
BUT HE'D JUST FORTIFIED HIMSELF TO DO BATTLE!
GREGOR HAD MORE BRAINS THAN BRAWN! BUT, THE HOMICIDAL GLEAM IN HIS EYE WASN'T THE SIGN OF A RATIONAL MAN!
SO, WHILE I WAS *KIND OF* TOUCHED BY THE HEROICS...
MOSTLY, I WAS SCARED...
...FOR THE STALKER!
STOP!
GREGOR, NO!!

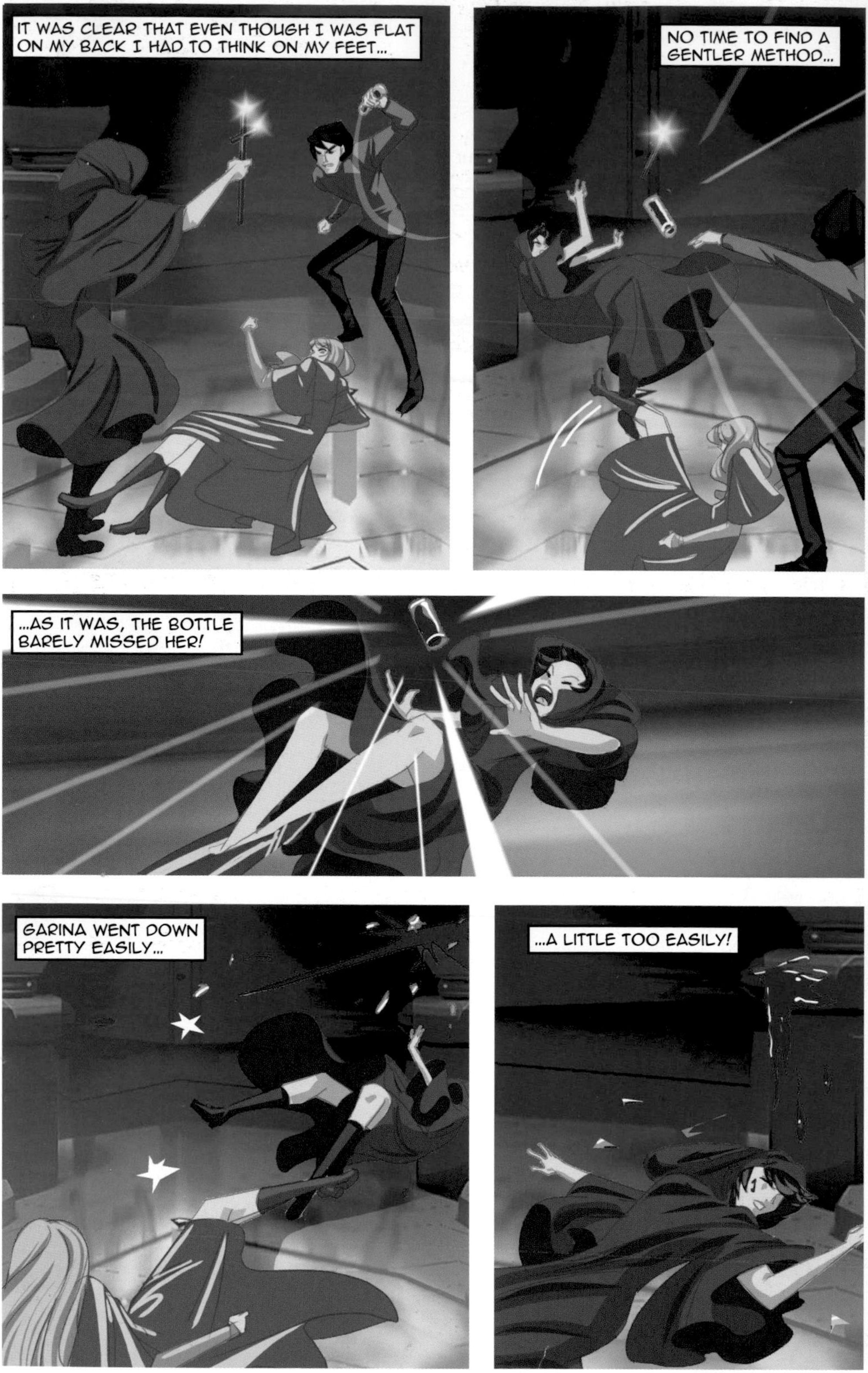
IT WAS CLEAR THAT EVEN THOUGH I WAS FLAT ON MY BACK I HAD TO THINK ON MY FEET...
NO TIME TO FIND A GENTLER METHOD...
...AS IT WAS, THE BOTTLE BARELY MISSED HER!
GARINA WENT DOWN PRETTY EASILY...
...A LITTLE TOO EASILY!

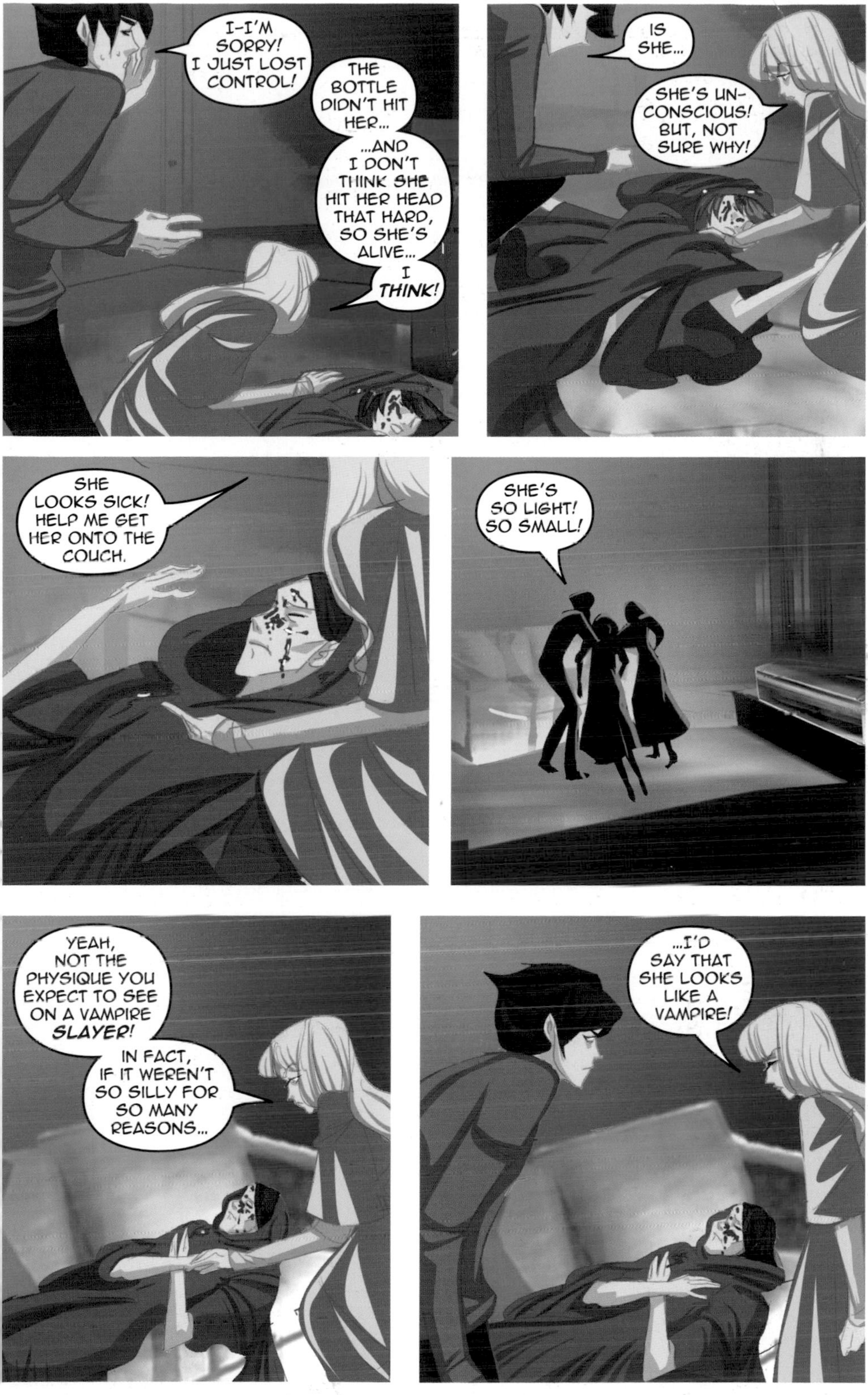
I-I'M SORRY! I JUST LOST CONTROL!
THE BOTTLE DIDN'T HIT HER...
...AND I DON'T THINK SHE HIT HER HEAD THAT HARD, SO SHE'S ALIVE...
I *THINK*!
IS SHE...
SHE'S UN-CONSCIOUS! BUT, NOT SURE WHY!
SHE LOOKS SICK! HELP ME GET HER ONTO THE COUCH.
SHE'S SO LIGHT! SO SMALL!
YEAH, NOT THE PHYSIQUE YOU EXPECT TO SEE ON A VAMPIRE *SLAYER*!
IN FACT, IF IT WEREN'T SO SILLY FOR SO MANY REASONS...
...I'D SAY THAT SHE LOOKS LIKE A VAMPIRE!

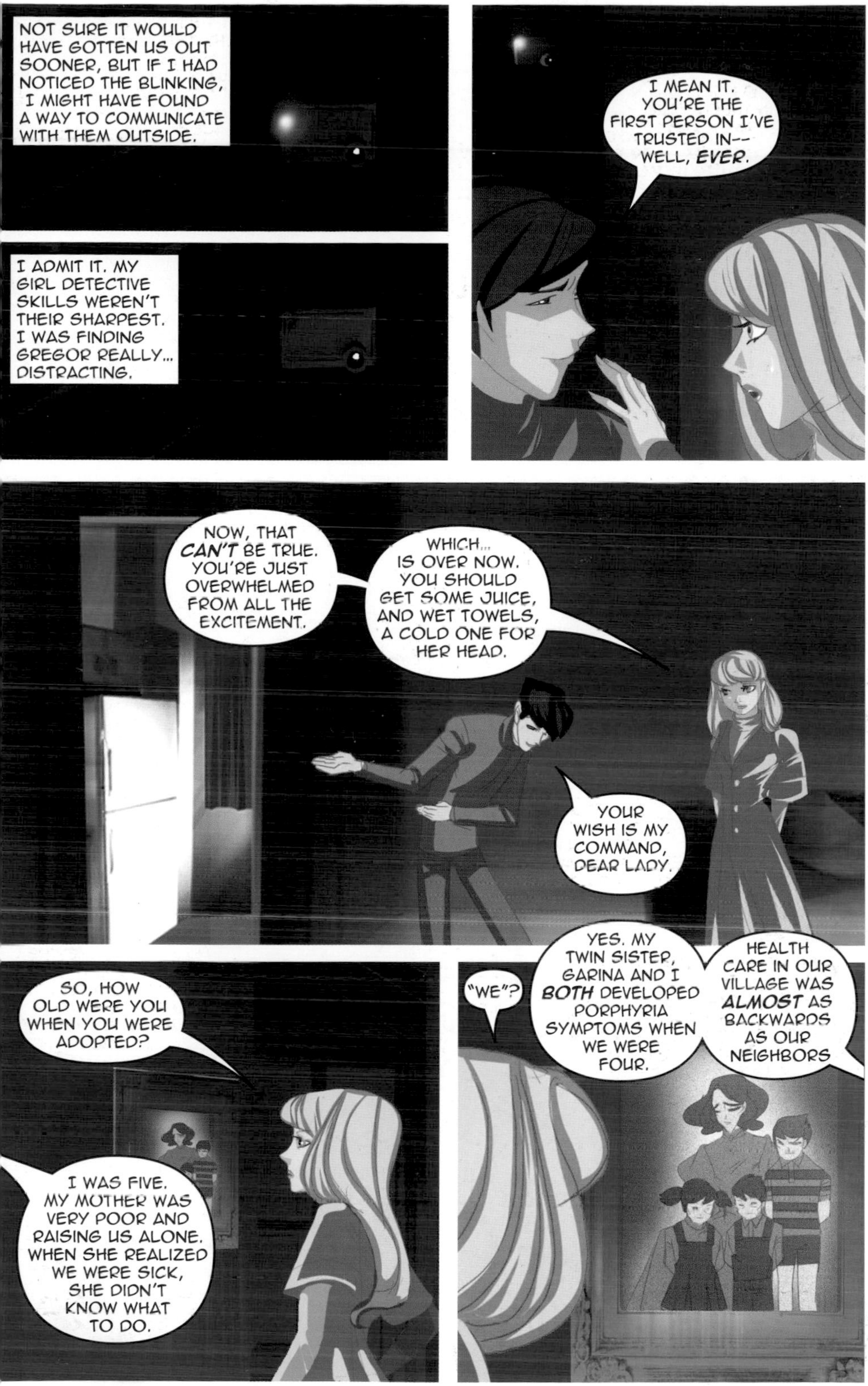
NOT SURE IT WOULD HAVE GOTTEN US OUT SOONER, BUT IF I HAD NOTICED THE BLINKING, I MIGHT HAVE FOUND A WAY TO COMMUNICATE WITH THEM OUTSIDE.
I ADMIT IT. MY GIRL DETECTIVE SKILLS WEREN'T THEIR SHARPEST. I WAS FINDING GREGOR REALLY... DISTRACTING.
I MEAN IT. YOU'RE THE FIRST PERSON I'VE TRUSTED IN-- WELL, *EVER*.
NOW, THAT *CAN'T* BE TRUE. YOU'RE JUST OVERWHELMED FROM ALL THE EXCITEMENT.
WHICH... IS OVER NOW. YOU SHOULD GET SOME JUICE, AND WET TOWELS, A COLD ONE FOR HER HEAD.
YOUR WISH IS MY COMMAND, DEAR LADY.
SO, HOW OLD WERE YOU WHEN YOU WERE ADOPTED?
I WAS FIVE. MY MOTHER WAS VERY POOR AND RAISING US ALONE. WHEN SHE REALIZED WE WERE SICK, SHE DIDN'T KNOW WHAT TO DO.
"WE"?
YES. MY TWIN SISTER, GARINA AND I *BOTH* DEVELOPED PORPHYRIA SYMPTOMS WHEN WE WERE FOUR.
HEALTH CARE IN OUR VILLAGE WAS *ALMOST* AS BACKWARDS AS OUR NEIGHBORS

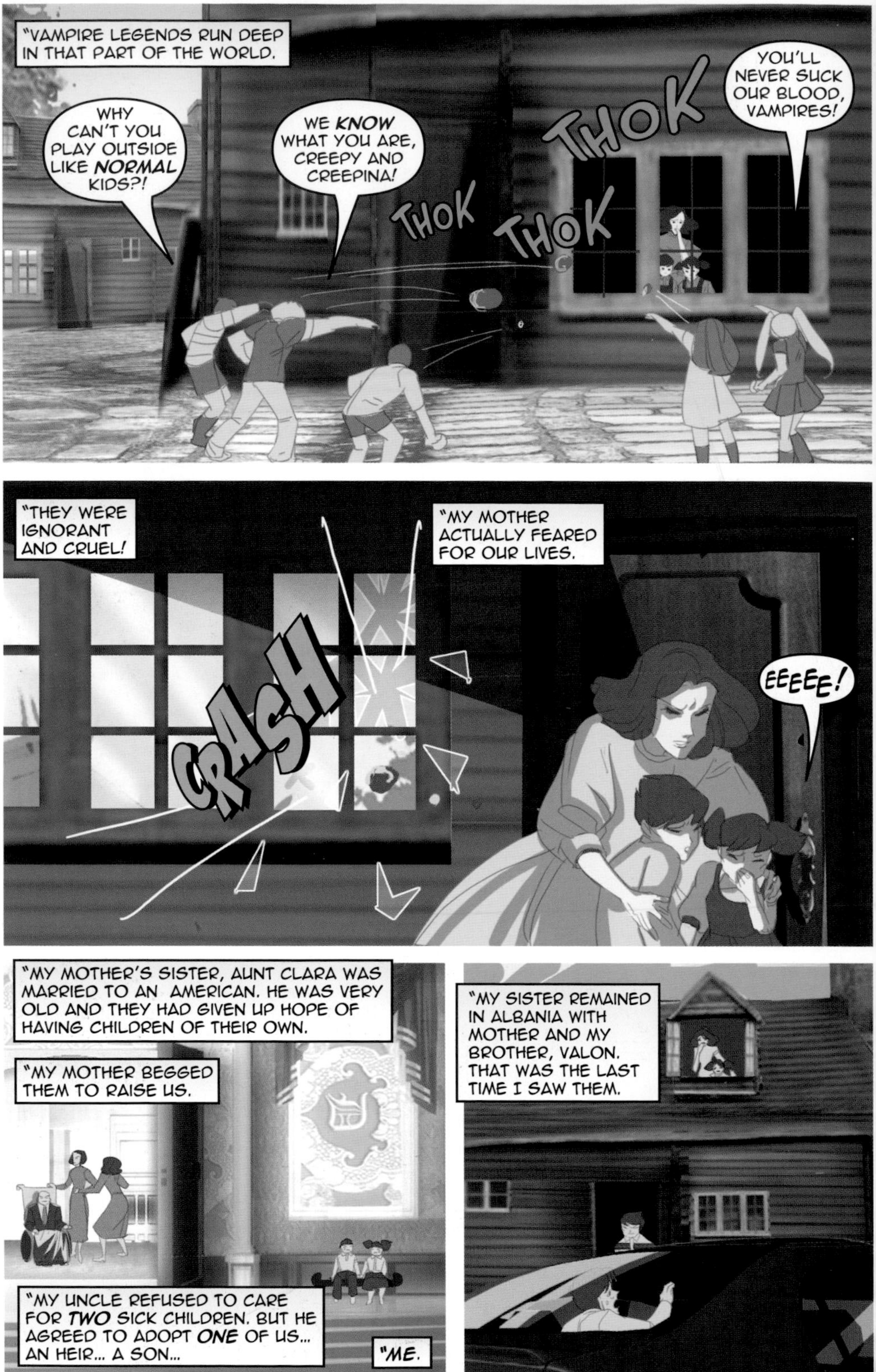
"VAMPIRE LEGENDS RUN DEEP IN THAT PART OF THE WORLD.
WHY CAN'T YOU PLAY OUTSIDE LIKE **NORMAL** KIDS?!
WE **KNOW** WHAT YOU ARE, CREEPY AND CREEPINA!
THOK
THOK
THOK
YOU'LL NEVER SUCK OUR BLOOD, VAMPIRES!
"THEY WERE IGNORANT AND CRUEL!
CRASH
"MY MOTHER ACTUALLY FEARED FOR OUR LIVES.
EEEEE!
"MY MOTHER'S SISTER, AUNT CLARA WAS MARRIED TO AN AMERICAN. HE WAS VERY OLD AND THEY HAD GIVEN UP HOPE OF HAVING CHILDREN OF THEIR OWN.
"MY MOTHER BEGGED THEM TO RAISE US.
"MY UNCLE REFUSED TO CARE FOR **TWO** SICK CHILDREN. BUT HE AGREED TO ADOPT **ONE** OF US... AN HEIR... A SON...
"**ME**.
"MY SISTER REMAINED IN ALBANIA WITH MOTHER AND MY BROTHER, VALON. THAT WAS THE LAST TIME I SAW THEM.

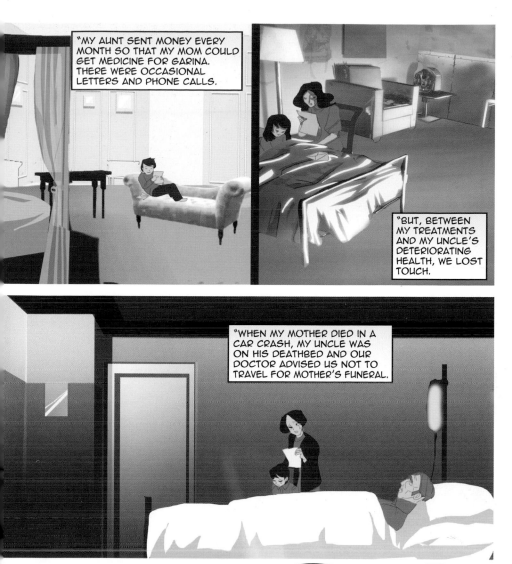

"MY AUNT SENT MONEY EVERY MONTH SO THAT MY MOM COULD GET MEDICINE FOR GARINA. THERE WERE OCCASIONAL LETTERS AND PHONE CALLS.

"BUT, BETWEEN MY TREATMENTS AND MY UNCLE'S DETERIORATING HEALTH, WE LOST TOUCH.

"WHEN MY MOTHER DIED IN A CAR CRASH, MY UNCLE WAS ON HIS DEATHBED AND OUR DOCTOR ADVISED US NOT TO TRAVEL FOR MOTHER'S FUNERAL.

"AFTER MY UNCLE DIED WE SENT FOR GARINA. BUT, THE LETTERS CAME BACK UNDELIVERED."

RETURN TO SENDER
ADDRESS UNKNOWN

AUNT CLARA INVESTIGATED, BUT NEVER FOUND GARINA OR VALON.

THEY SAY TWINS HAVE A SPECIAL BOND. BUT, I HAVE NO SENSE OF GARINA BEING ALIVE OR... NOT. I MAY NEVER KNOW.

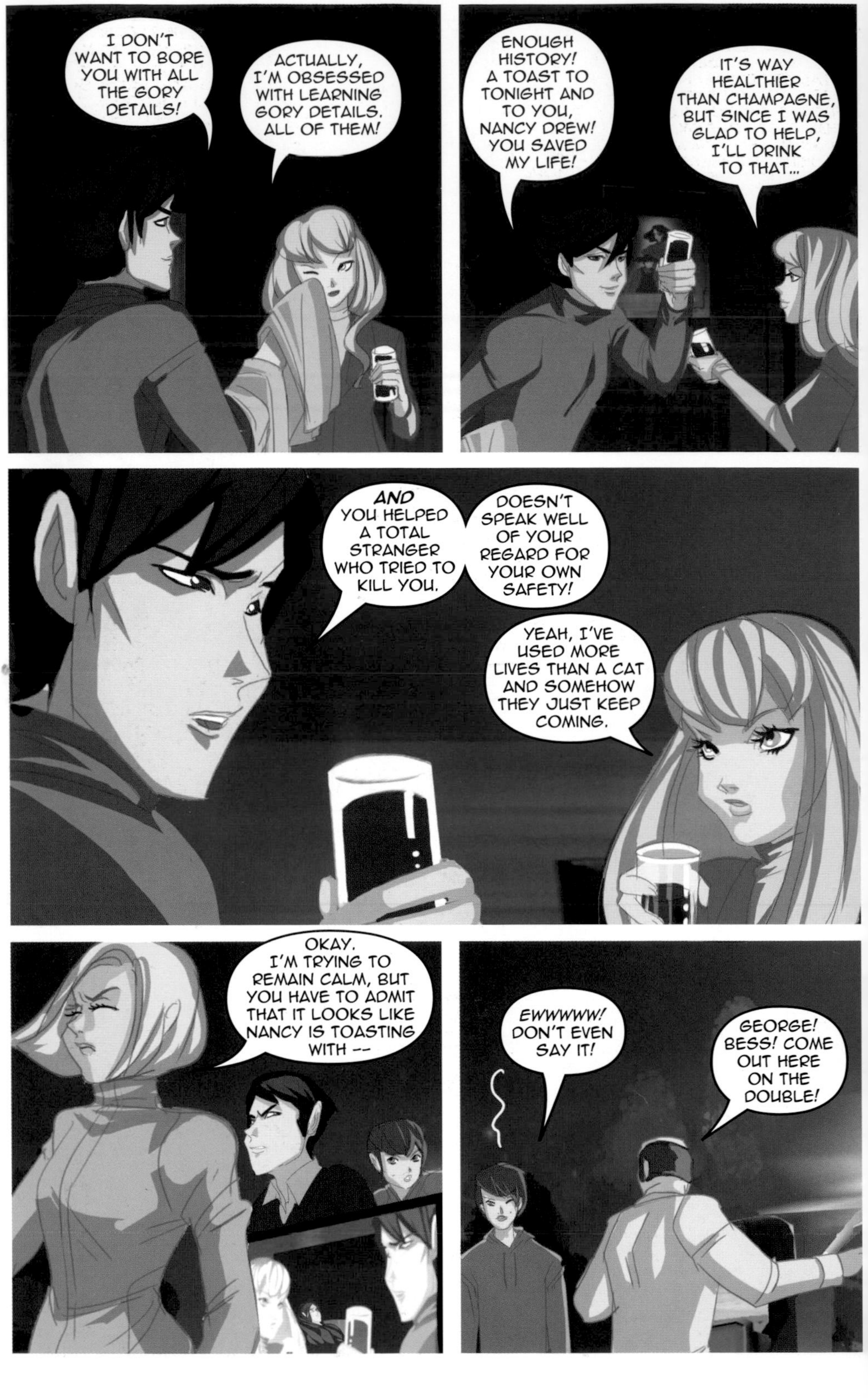
I DON'T WANT TO BORE YOU WITH ALL THE GORY DETAILS!
ACTUALLY, I'M OBSESSED WITH LEARNING GORY DETAILS. ALL OF THEM!
ENOUGH HISTORY! A TOAST TO TONIGHT AND TO YOU, NANCY DREW! YOU SAVED MY LIFE!
IT'S WAY HEALTHIER THAN CHAMPAGNE, BUT SINCE I WAS GLAD TO HELP, I'LL DRINK TO THAT...
AND YOU HELPED A TOTAL STRANGER WHO TRIED TO KILL YOU.
DOESN'T SPEAK WELL OF YOUR REGARD FOR YOUR OWN SAFETY!
YEAH, I'VE USED MORE LIVES THAN A CAT AND SOMEHOW THEY JUST KEEP COMING.
OKAY. I'M TRYING TO REMAIN CALM, BUT YOU HAVE TO ADMIT THAT IT LOOKS LIKE NANCY IS TOASTING WITH --
EWWWWW! DON'T EVEN SAY IT!
GEORGE! BESS! COME OUT HERE ON THE DOUBLE!

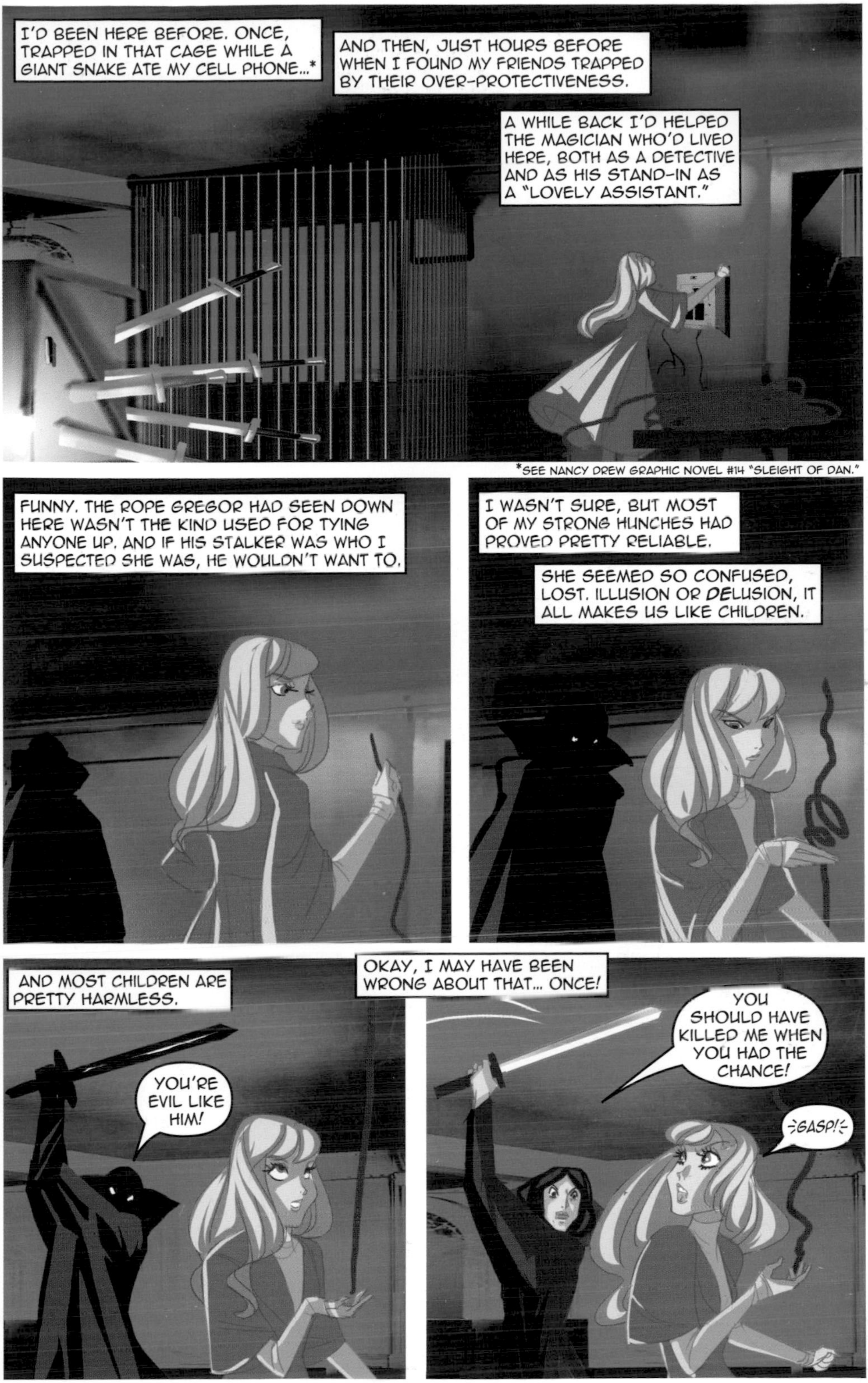

I'D BEEN HERE BEFORE. ONCE, TRAPPED IN THAT CAGE WHILE A GIANT SNAKE ATE MY CELL PHONE...*
AND THEN, JUST HOURS BEFORE WHEN I FOUND MY FRIENDS TRAPPED BY THEIR OVER-PROTECTIVENESS.
A WHILE BACK I'D HELPED THE MAGICIAN WHO'D LIVED HERE, BOTH AS A DETECTIVE AND AS HIS STAND-IN AS A "LOVELY ASSISTANT."
*SEE NANCY DREW GRAPHIC NOVEL #14 "SLEIGHT OF DAN."
FUNNY. THE ROPE GREGOR HAD SEEN DOWN HERE WASN'T THE KIND USED FOR TYING ANYONE UP. AND IF HIS STALKER WAS WHO I SUSPECTED SHE WAS, HE WOULDN'T WANT TO.
I WASN'T SURE, BUT MOST OF MY STRONG HUNCHES HAD PROVED PRETTY RELIABLE.
SHE SEEMED SO CONFUSED, LOST. ILLUSION OR DELUSION, IT ALL MAKES US LIKE CHILDREN.
AND MOST CHILDREN ARE PRETTY HARMLESS.
YOU'RE EVIL LIKE HIM!
OKAY, I MAY HAVE BEEN WRONG ABOUT THAT... ONCE!
YOU SHOULD HAVE KILLED ME WHEN YOU HAD THE CHANCE!
GASP!

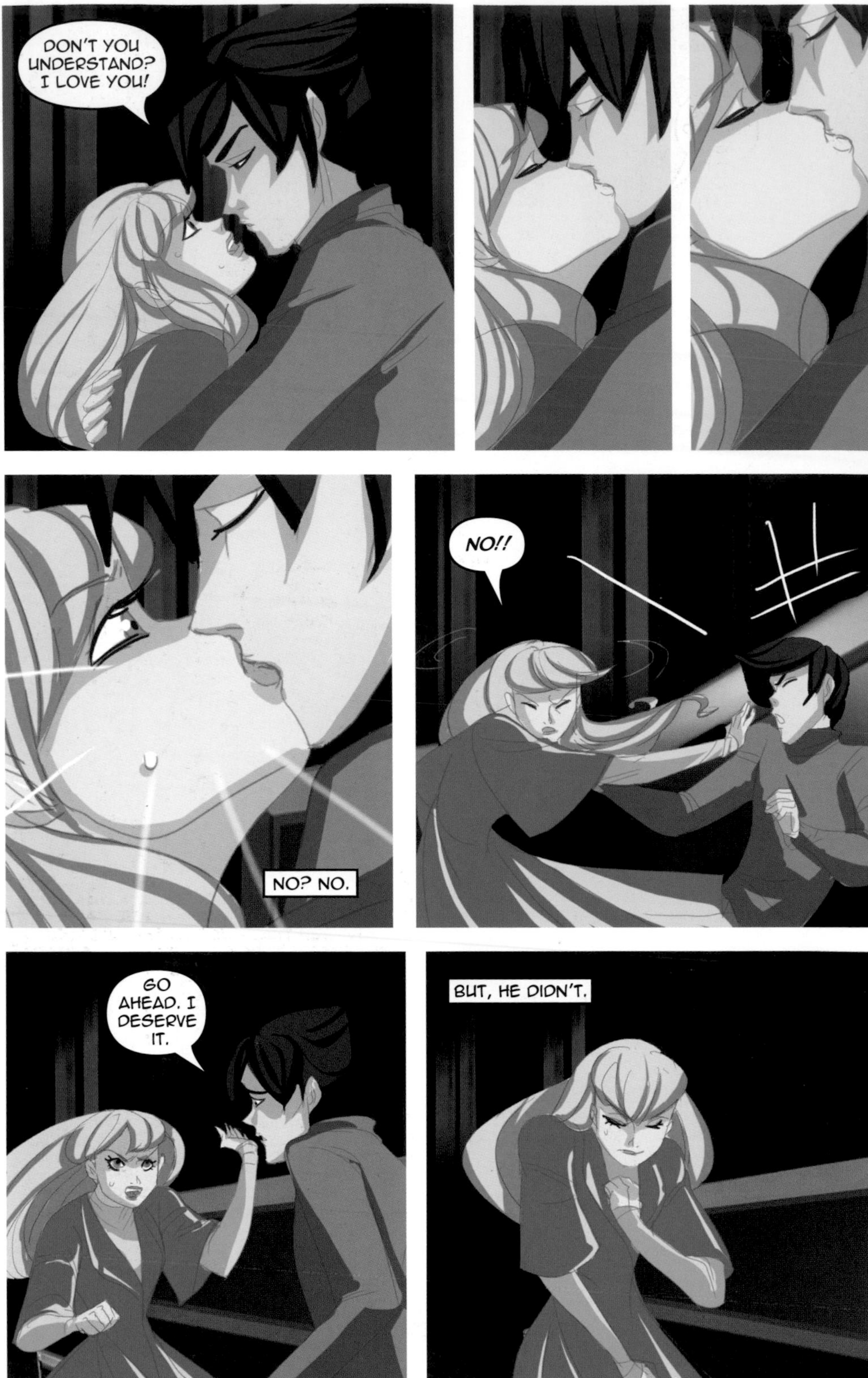
DON'T YOU UNDERSTAND? I LOVE YOU!
NO? NO.
NO!!
GO AHEAD. I DESERVE IT.
BUT, HE DIDN'T.

NANCY DREW GRAPHIC NOVELS AVAILABLE FROM PAPERCUTZ

NEW STORY! FULL-COLOR GRAPHIC NOVEL

NANCY·DREW GIRL DETECTIVE

CLIFFHANGER

Based on the series by Carolyn Keene

Stefan Petrucha & Sarah Kinney
Sho Murase & Carlos Guzman

PAPERCUT Z

#19 "Cliffhanger"

#12 "Dress Reversal"

#13 "Doggone Town"

#14 "Sleight of Dan"

#15 "Tiger Counter"

#16 "What Goes Up..."

#17 "Night of the Living Chatchke"

#18 "City Under the Basement"

#20 "High School Musical Mystery" 1

#21 "High School Musical Mystery" 2

The New Case Files #1 "Vampire Slayer" Part 1

Graphic Novels #12-19 are $7.95 in paperback, $12.95 hardcover. Graphic Novels #20 and #21 are $8.99 in paperback, $13.99 hardcover. NANCY DREW The New Case Files #1 is $6.99 in paperback, $10.99 hardcover. Please add $4.00 for postage and handling for the first book, add $1.00 for each additional book.
Please make check payable to NBM Publishing. Send to:
Papercutz, 1200 County Rd. Rte. 523, Flemington, NJ 08822, 1-800-886-1223
www.papercutz.com

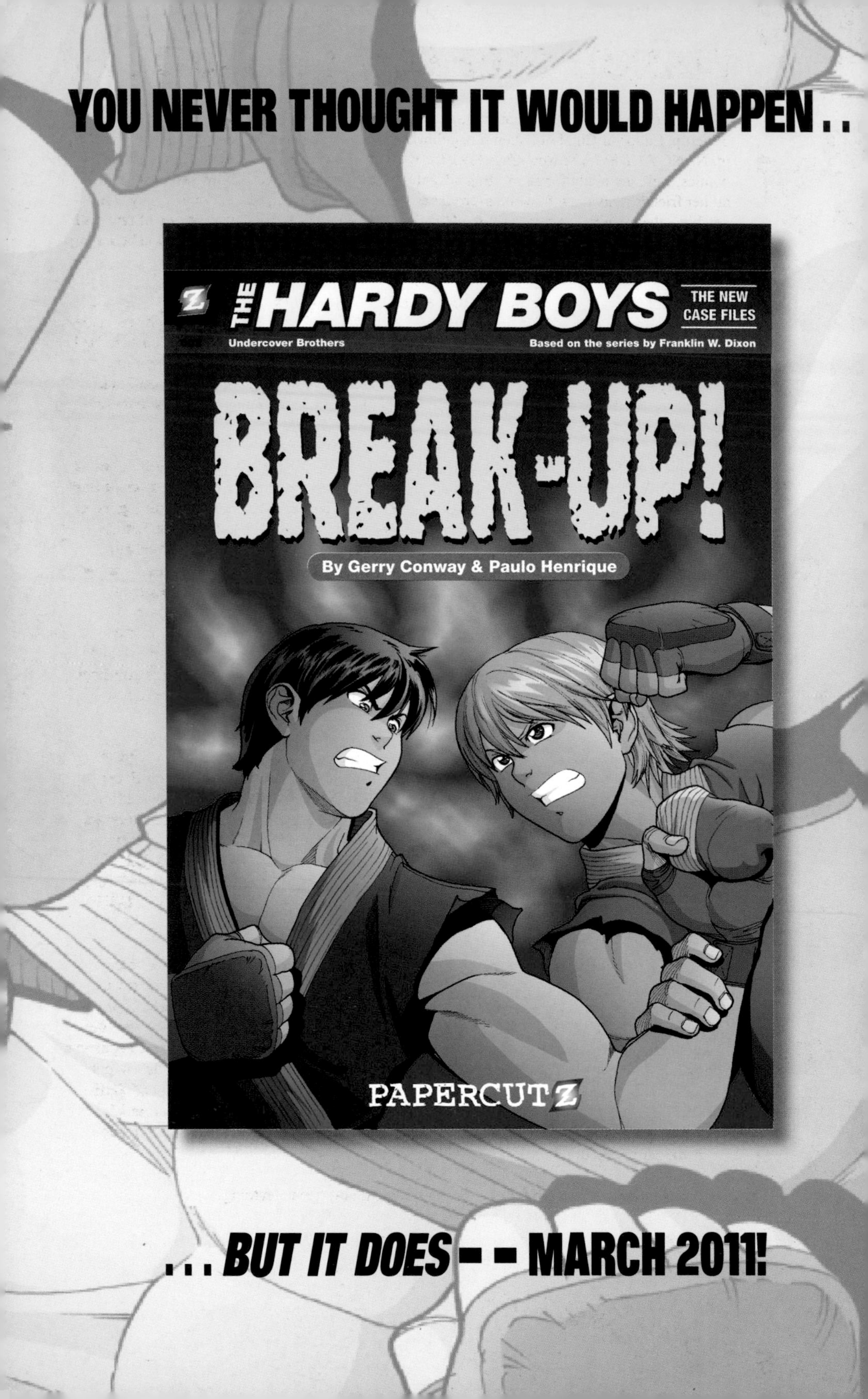
YOU NEVER THOUGHT IT WOULD HAPPEN..
THE HARDY BOYS
THE NEW CASE FILES
Undercover Brothers
Based on the series by Franklin W. Dixon
BREAK-UP!
By Gerry Conway & Paulo Henrique
PAPERCUTZ
...BUT IT DOES -- MARCH 2011!

WATCH OUT FOR PAPERCUTZ ™

Welcome to the second edition of the all-new NANCY DREW graphic novel series! I'm Jim Salicrup, Editor-in-Chief of Papercutz, publisher of graphic novels for all-ages. If you picked up NANCY DREW The New Case Files #1, welcome back! If you're new to Nancy Drew comics, well, get ready for an exciting adventure featuring your favorite Girl Detective and all her friends (and a few frenemies) from her prose series. And if you're a total Nancy Drew newbie—then you're about to meet the Girl Detective who has thrilled generations of fans with her sleuthing skills, and her insatiable desire to solve mysteries. I suspect you'll soon be falling in love with Nancy Drew too!

Speaking of loving Nancy Drew, (SPOILER ALERT—skip to next paragraph if you haven't yet read "Vampire Slayer" Part Two!), what do you think of the surprising developments in the chilling conclusion to "Vampire Slayer"?! Did you ever think you'd see anyone other than Ned Nickerson kissing Nancy Drew? And what about Ned hooking up with Deirdre Shannon…? Obviously there's a lot of unexpected events going on in River Heights these days, and that leads us to the news many of you have been waiting for ever since Nancy Drew first appeared in her own series of graphic novels! Read on…

If you picked up THE HARDY BOYS The New Case Files #1 "Crawling with Zombies" or #2 "Break Up!" then you'll know that strange things have also been happening in the town of Bayport! First, Undercover Brothers Frank and Joe Hardy encounter a bizarre plot involving teens disguised as zombies, and as a result of conflicting crime-fighting styles, the two A.T.A.C. (American Teens Against Crime) agents decide they no longer want to work together! How unbelievable is that?! The Hardy Boys have been a team—like forever! Can they really being going their separate ways? Well, yes—and that leads us to our biggest announcement yet!

Frank and Joe Hardy are now convinced, based on all the clues they've uncovered, that the mastermind behind all the recent weirdness in Bayport is in the town of River Heights—and that they need to go there to find answers. And if you guessed that that means The Hardy Boys will be co-starring in NANCY DREW The New Case Files #3 "Together With The Hardy Boys," then you are correct!

Yes, it's true! Ever since we started publishing the Papercutz HARDY BOYS and NANCY DREW graphic novels, you have been demanding that we publish an adventure with Frank, Joe, and Nancy together! We held out because we really wanted to make it something extra-special! After all, The Hardys and Miss Drew have worked together numerous times in books and on TV in the past, and we wanted to do something a little different. This time, Nancy is caught between Frank and Joe Hardy, who no longer want to work together, (ANOTHER SPOILER WARNING! Skip to next paragraph if you haven't yet read "Vampire Slayer" Part Two!) at a time when she may be split with Ned! Maybe we should've titled NANCY DREW The New Case Files #3 "It's Complicated!"

As exciting as that HARDY BOYS/NANCY DREW bombshell may be—there's still other amazing graphic novels being published by Papercutz as well! You may've heard about an all-new, blockbuster 3-D Smurfs movie coming to a theater near you August 3rd, 2011, or maybe you enjoy the Smurfs cartoons on the Boomerang channel! But did you know that the Smurfs first appeared in comics? They were created by the great cartoonist Peyo, and Papercutz is proud to now be publishing those classic comics in THE SMURFS graphic novels! To get a small sample of smurfy goodness, just check out the next few pages for a preview of THE SMURFS Graphic Novel #3 "The Smurf King"! You may be surprised to discover that it's more sophisticated than you might have thought! Be sure to check out the whole story, and enjoy the satire and fun.

That's more than enough for now. So, until next time—keep sleuthing!

JiM

© Peyo - 2010 - Licensed through Lafig Belgium - www.smurf.com

Get the complete story in THE SMURFS Graphic Novel #3 "The Smurf King" available at booksellers everywhere!

NOW AVAILABLE IN BOXED SETS...

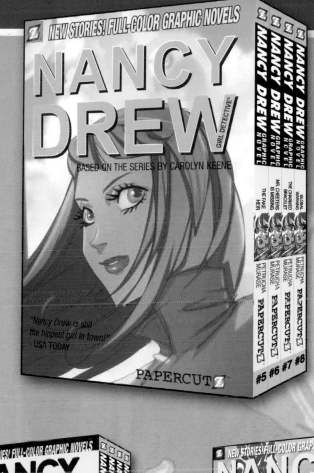

ON SALE AT BOOKSELLERS EVERYWHERE!

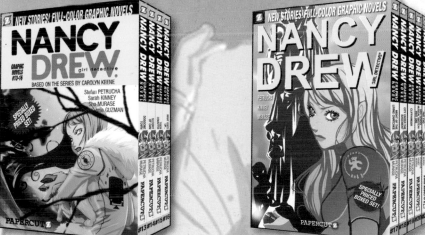

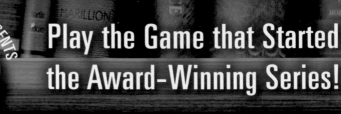

HER INTERACTIVE PRESENTS
NANCY DREW
80th ANNIVERSARY
1930 — 2010

Play the Game that Started the Award-Winning Series!

NANCY DREW®
SECRETS CAN KILL!

REMASTERED!
Brand New Ending
3D Animated Characters
Challenging New Puzzles

dare to play®

WIN/MAC CD-ROM

AUGUST 2010 • Order at HerInteractive.com or call 1-800-461-8787. Also in stores!

RATING PENDING ™
RP
Visit www.esrb.org
for rating information
ESRB CONTENT RATING   www.esrb.org

Copyright © 2010 Her Interactive, Inc. HER INTERACTIVE, the HER INTERACTIVE logo and DARE TO PLAY are trademarks of Her Interactive, Inc. NANCY DREW is a trademark of Simon & Schuster, Inc. and is used under license. Copyright in the NANCY DREW books and characters are owned by Simon & Schuster, Inc. All rights reserved. Licensed by permission of Simon & Schuster, Inc. Other brands or product names are trademarks of their respective holders.

HeR
INTERACTIVE